Murder in The Vatican
THE CHURCH MYSTERIES OF SHERLOCK HOLMES

ALL THREE OF US PLACED OURSELVES AT OUTER EDGE OF THE ROOM
WHILE HOLMES EXAMINED THE GRIM SCENE, SCOURING IT WITH
HIS HAWK-LIKE GAZE.

Page 16.

Murder in The Vatican

The Church Mysteries of Sherlock Holmes

By
ANN MARGARET LEWIS

Illustrated by Rikki Niehaus

Gasogene Books
INDIANAPOLIS

GASOGENE BOOKS
An imprint of Wessex Press, LLC
P.O. Box 68308
Indianapolis, IN 46268

Father Brown, Flambeau and all related characters created by G.K. Chesterton, used with the permission of the Royal Literary Fund.

ISBN 978-0-938501-52-7

Printed in the United States of America.

1 3 5 7 6 4 2

First Edition

In memory of my mother
MARY ANN GOETZ
who once told me
"If you can read, you can do anything."

Contents

Murder in The Vatican

THE CHURCH MYSTERIES OF SHERLOCK HOLMES

The Death of Cardinal Tosca

"In this memorable year '95 a curious an incongruous succession of cases had engaged his attention, ranging from his famous investigation of the sudden death of Cardinal Tosca — an inquiry which was carried out by him at the express desire of His Holiness the Pope...."

— DR. JOHN H. WATSON,
"The Adventure of Black Peter"

T HE YEAR 1895 was perhaps the most productive in the career of my dear friend Mr. Sherlock Holmes. The previous year he had dramatically returned from a three-year absence during which I and all of London believed he'd perished with the late Professor Moriarty at Reichenbach Falls. This resurrection only served to increase the demand for his unparalleled skills, and from April '94 to April of '95, he was engaged on at least one new case a month, bringing each of them to a successful and often remarkable conclusion.

Such a pace did not seem to place an excessive strain on his constitution and I was not, as yet, overly concerned for his health as I had cause to be in the past. Still, for his sake as well as for my own desire for a change, I began, not long after March had ended, to put forward the idea of a brief holiday. Sadly, he rejected my suggestion, concentrating on who or what might next appear on our doorstep.

But approaching the height of May, there was a sudden dearth of clients to challenge my friend's unique faculties. I realised it was probably a natural lull in business, but the absence of interesting problems made Holmes irritable. Hoping to improve his mood, I once more made my proposal for a holiday since it would be the perfect time to be away. Once again Holmes brushed aside my comment with a gruff murmur, deciding instead to fill his time by organising the voluminous piles of paper on his desk. Over several days this only made our rooms increasingly more cluttered as he sorted sheets on the floor, mantel, tables, spare chairs, and other flat surfaces, forcing me to navigate skilfully over and around them like a Chinese acrobat.

As we sat at breakfast on a stuffy, overcast day with the promise of more heat to come, I folded my copy of the *Times* over to a story on the declining health of Louis Pasteur, a man Holmes and I both admired. I'd just started to consider that perhaps a visit to the continent might stir Holmes' interest when Mrs. Hudson, stepping gracefully around Holmes' many document stacks, handed Holmes a buff-coloured envelope addressed to him.

"Delivered this minute, by commissionaire, Mr. Holmes."

He studied the envelope, then opened it with a curious expression. "From the London offices of our friend Mr. John Vincent Harden. Thank you, Mrs. Hudson, and if you would be so good as to remove the small remains of the most excellent breakfast you provided us, we shall see what Mr. Harden has to tell us." Holmes removed the single sheet the envelope contained and glanced over it. "Ah—this is forwarded by his London office, for he writes to me from Italy." He chuckled.

I lowered my paper. "Something amusing, Holmes?" I asked.

"Something unexpected, at least," he replied. "Watson, if in the near future you were planning to suggest once more a break in our work, please do not trouble yourself. It appears Mr. Harden is of a like mind. What would you say to a week or two in a Roman villa?"

"I'd say it would be unexpected, indeed," I replied. I took the letter he passed to me and read it.

Dear Mr. Holmes,

I hope this letter finds you well—certainly as well as I after your assistance. After my trying experiences last month, I decided to spend time with my family in my summer villa outside Rome, not far from Castel Gandolfo. Since we last met, I've reflected long on my debt to you for restoring peace to my life. As a further sign of my gratitude, I would like to extend to you and Dr. Watson an invitation to stay a few weeks on continental holiday at my villa here, this month or perhaps the next. The Roman hills are quite pleasant now, and I am certain we can find enough activity (or inactivity, if either of you prefer it), to suit your desires.

If this suggestion meets with your approval and that of the good doctor, please reply by wire through my London office so I can arrange transport from Calais via my private train. It will provide the amenities for you both for the two days' journey to Rome, where I can play the host more directly. I await your reply and hope to see you both again in the near future.

Yours,

JOHN VINCENT HARDEN

"Good heavens," I said. "Hasn't he compensated you enough?"

"He was certainly generous," Holmes agreed. "But it would appear he feels he has not adequately expressed his gratitude. Well, Watson, what say you? Ah—I can read the answer in your face before you give it without any use of those talents you attribute to me so generously. Here is your wished for holiday, *gratis*. Can London really spare the two of us? Shall it be *Roma?*"

I glanced at the letter in my hand once more, then back at him with, I fear, an eager smile. "You know, I've never been to Rome. Nor have I ever enjoyed a private train."

"And I wonder which weighed the more heavily in the scales. Very well, old friend. I'll send a reply accepting this afternoon. We shall both require time to tidy up loose ends." He gestured to the litter surrounding his chair. "Perhaps the first week in June? Will that give you time to secure a *locum tenens?*"

"Jackson has always been accommodating in that regard. I'll speak to him to-day."

And so, by the end of the first week in June, Holmes and I were on the ferry to Calais where we met Harden's private train. It was a splendid glossy black engine with yellow touches, and four coaches to match. One coach was a sleeping car for passengers with several separate sleeping compartments all served by a porter. The second car was an elegant dining car staffed by a chef and two servers. A third had an elegant sitting room with a small library served by a butler, and the final car provided sleeping quarters for the servants.

While the porter placed my bags in the first sleeping compartment, I strolled back through the cars. Halfway through the train, I saw Holmes standing outside the dining car speaking with the engineer and fireman. I stepped out to join their conversation.

"We'll be making stops, of course," said the engineer, "But only to discard waste and take on coal and water. Everything you'll need is here on board and you need only ask. If you do wish to stop somewhere, simply have the porter bring a note to us."

"Marvellous." Holmes looked to me with a mischievous twinkle in his eyes. "Since we'll be passing through the Swiss Alps, why don't we stop in Meiringen and take in Reichenbach Falls. Just for the memories?"

I frowned. "Don't even joke about it."

He rested a firm hand on my shoulder. "I wasn't serious, old friend." He turned to the engineer. "Thank you for the offer, but we prefer to go straight to Rome."

The engineer touched his hat and motioned to the fireman to follow him to the front, and we were underway. For all of two days we enjoyed the exquisite cuisine provided by Mr. Harden's chef, enjoyed some superb vintages and smoked first-class tobacco produced by Harden's company in America. It was, in my opinion, the most pleasant trip of my life.

By the time we reached Harden's train depot outside Rome early in the morning, my friend and I were well-rested, well-fed and enthusiastic about finding fresh adventures.

"Well, Watson, I believe a problem has already found us," Holmes said as the train rolled to a stop at the platform.

"Why do you say that, Holmes?"

He pointed out the window. "Observe the priest with Harden outside. Harden is a Catholic convert, but I'd hardly expect him bring along a priest to greet us, let alone one who obviously works at the Vatican. And this one looks particularly

6

anxious. He was in such a hurry to come he didn't button his cassock properly; the buttons are misaligned."

"The Vatican?" I saw the young man in his mid twenties with Harden, wearing a clerical collar and a long, black, buttoned cassock, bouncing nervously on his toes. He was a thin youth with dark hair, and his large brown eyes searched the cars with a worried gaze. "Do you believe he's from the Vatican because he has the pallor of one who spends more time indoors rather than out in the Italian sun among his parishioners?"

"Not at all, Watson. A parish priest could be just as pale and spend as much time indoors." Holmes stood and put on his hat. "The anxiety is obvious, but he is clearly employed at the Vatican. Did you not observe that in his right hand he is clutching a linen paper envelope sealed with red wax, stamped with an ornate seal? Who else but the Pope would send a priest with such a letter?"

I blinked out the window. The young man had turned to walk down the platform so I could not see his hands. "Are you certain—?" I stood and followed Holmes from the car.

Holmes did not answer. He stepped briskly from the train waving to Harden. "Ho! Mr. Harden!"

John Vincent Harden, Sr. was a hardy American from North Carolina who'd taken an Italian heiress as a wife. Standing near six feet tall, his was a shocking presence with his red-brown hair and close-trimmed beard. Beaming, he greeted each of us with a firm handshake. "Mr. Holmes, Dr. Watson—good to see you both again." He leaned in close and whispered, "I'm afraid I've made a mistake."

"What's that?" Holmes said, with a mildly amused smile.

"When I told my wife you were coming, she in turn told her friends, who told their friends—"

"So now all of Roman society knows we're here."

"I'm afraid so." Harden's lips turned downward. "Of course, dinner invitations have come and such—"

"And—?"

"And this young priest arrived today from the Vatican seeking your help. I tried to explain that you were coming to visit on holiday, but he was very insistent. Then he told me he'd come from the Holy Father himself—"

Holmes clapped his hands. "Ha! What did I say, Watson?" He rubbed his palms together eagerly.

"His Holiness must have appreciated your work with the cameos," I said, "to ask for you again."

"Cameos?" Harden asked.

"A singular issue of missing valuable artworks at the Vatican seven years ago. I was honoured to meet His Holiness at the time. He impressed me greatly."

Harden released a wry laugh. "I'm the Catholic here and I haven't had the honour of meeting the man."

"I haven't met him either," said I. "Holmes took that case without me."

"I suspect that will all be remedied soon." Holmes looked pointedly at Harden. "That is if you're to join us."

"Me?" Harden's eyes widened with surprise. "I don't know how much help I'd be."

"You're fluent in Italian?"

"My wife wouldn't tolerate less."

"We will need your expertise. His Holiness speaks French, so communicating with him is no trouble. My Italian is passable enough to communicate with others, but I do believe my friend here may need some assistance in that regard."

"The extent of my Italian is from opera," I said with chagrin. "I could see you being a great help."

"The idea of joining you on a case that isn't about me is an exciting proposition," Harden said as he escorted us down the platform. "I'll help you in any way I can."

"Another pair of eyes and ears is always beneficial as well, as Watson knows. Now introduce us to the lad before he wears a hole in the platform."

The young clergyman had walked to the end of train to give us privacy. He was pacing back and forth reading his breviary.

"Father Dionisio!" Harden beckoned to the priest, who looked up and rushed to meet us with his free hand outstretched.

8

"*Signori, piacere!*" He said, he closed the small book one-handed and stuffed it in his pocket. "Signore Holmes?" He asked, gripping Holmes' hand.

"Yes, and this is Dr. Watson," Holmes said, indicating me.

He shook my hand as well. "*Dottore, piacere, piacere.*"

"The porter already has your bags at the carriage," Harden said. "I'll have him send them home and we can take my train into Rome proper. Once we get underway, we'll be there in ten minutes."

"Excellent," said Holmes. "We can listen to Father Dionisio's tale as we go."

"I will tell the engineer to telegraph ahead for the points to be set. Make yourselves comfortable in the leisure car."

Harden translated this quickly for the priest who nodded eagerly, and we boarded the train together. Harden joined us promptly and the train set off for Rome.

From this point on, most of our conversations were conducted in Italian. Thankfully, Mr. Harden proved a very capable interpreter. His translation was smooth, quiet and synchronous, hardly impeding on the conversation at all. He was also a font of information on the traditions and trappings of the Church, having studied it a good deal before his conversion. After the case, he reminded me of all that transpired so I could write an accurate and detailed chronicle.

Father Dionisio produced from the pages of his breviary the small white envelope sealed in red wax that Holmes saw earlier and handed it to my friend. Holmes opened it and read the single page it contained with a slight smile curling the edge of his lips.

"Father Dionisio, please tell us the sum of the problem," he said putting the letter in his jacket pocket. "His Holiness writes that it is quite suspicious."

"The Holy Father suspects it is murder, Signore."

Holmes' expression darkened. He leaned his elbows on the arms of his chair and pressed the tips his fingers together. "Pray continue."

"This morning, Cardinal Tosca, the newly appointed Cardinal Prefect of Rites for the Roman Curia, was found dead in his office. One moment he was perfectly healthy, the next he was slumped over his writing desk dead."

"Did His Eminence have a weak heart?" I asked. "Any breathing problems? Any fatigue to speak of?"

Dionisio shook his head. "For forty-two years, he was as healthy as a thoroughbred race horse. He took frequent long walks and enjoyed mountain hiking during his holidays."

"Had His Eminence taken any food that morning?" Holmes asked.

"Coffee with milk and a hard roll. His secretary brought the cardinal's breakfast to him from the seminarians' dining room where the secretary himself had eaten."

Holmes rubbed his chin thoughtfully. "Continue."

"The truly odd thing was that he was visited right after breakfast by a young woman who'd been brought to the cardinal's secretary after she pleaded with the Captain of the Guard to see him about a matter of urgency and scandal. Cardinal Tosca's secretary, Brother Michele Finoglio, a Jesuit seminarian as I said, presented her card to His Eminence and he received her. The cardinal's nephew, Giuseppe Tosca, an art student at the public school of cameo artisans, arrived a few minutes later. He entered His Eminence's suite and then, at the request of Cardinal Tosca, escorted the girl to the street. Brother Michele said she was weeping terribly when she left. Giuseppe claims he hailed a cab for her, but he doesn't know where she went from there. After Giuseppe left, Brother Michele went into the room and found His Eminence dead. He quickly alerted the guard and His Holiness."

"Does the secretary remember the woman's name?"

"He could not remember it precisely, nor could he find the card she sent in. It was nowhere to be found on His Eminence's person or on his desk."

"Puzzling," Holmes said. "Of course, I may find it when we inspect the cardinal's suite."

"The Holy Father remembered how you valued an untouched crime scene, Signore. He ordered a guard placed on the room with the door locked, leaving the body as it was so you might see all that you can."

"His Holiness is wise."

"Of course, we can't leave His Eminence that way for too long," Dionisio said. "That is the reason for our urgency."

"Then I say we make all haste. I believe we've reached our stop."

The warm sun, now high in the morning sky, gleamed upon the huge, white dome of St. Peter's Basilica as our carriage made its way between spraying fountains into the vast piazza of St. Peter. Along the ivory-pillared colonnade that flanked the church and the massive cathedral edifice itself, the statues of saints shone as gold in the eastern light, casting lengthy shadows along the cobblestone pavement. Far in the sky beyond the dome, however, I saw smoky dark clouds that foreshadowed an impending rainstorm, and a dull ache in my old war injury confirmed the threat.

Beyond the colonnade we passed through a series of arched gates guarded by Swiss Guardsmen in their red, blue, and yellow sixteenth century-style uniforms and alighted from our carriage in the enclosed Courtyard of St. Damasus within the Apostolic Palace walls. Father Dionisio moved ahead of us to speak to the imposing soldiers, two of whom stood on either side of door with halberds at the ready. Dionisio spoke to a third tall soldier, apparently the commanding officer, who carried no pole arm but wore a sword and pistol at his side. When he nodded and motioned for us to come forward, we followed Dionisio through the entryway and into the cool, ivory marble hall.

Dionisio took a silver pocket watch from his right pocket and glanced at it. "The Holy Father should be just finishing his morning Mass in his private chapel. It was greatly delayed due to the incident. He said if at all possible he would prefer to accompany us to the cardinal's suite."

"Shouldn't we go straight to the scene?" I asked.

I saw a flash of uncertainty in the young man's eyes at the suggestion. "His Holiness was very insistent. If he were at the beginning of Mass I'd say yes, but since he's at the end we should go to him first. He's cleared his entire schedule for the day to attend to this situation."

Dionisio walked swiftly, leading us up two long flights of massive marble stairs to papal reception rooms on the second floor. The walls on either side of us were illustrated with rich, colourful frescoes which I sadly had no time to study as we progressed. Upon entering the papal reception rooms, we first stepped through a large guard room staffed by Papal Guard to whom Dionisio said a few quick words. He then ushered us into a small sitting room. At the end of this room was a single white door, also secured by guardsmen. Dionisio held the door open for us and we stepped then into the sacred silence of the Pope's private chapel.

There were only a few other people present in the small, renaissance-styled chapel, three or four lay people and three other men in clerical attire. Dionisio genuflected and led us around to the right side of the chapel, where he slid into the front pews to the right of the altar and the Pope's back. He gestured for us to kneel as he did. The Mass was ending, and while I was impressed by the pageantry of ritual and vesture, I fear I was a bit confounded by it. I later asked Harden to explain to me all I'd seen, and he happily obliged.

The pontiff, Leo XIII, was kneeling facing the altar flanked by two acolytes in black albs with white surplices. He was vested in ornate, embroidered silk green and gold vestments under which was an elegant lace alb. From where I knelt, I could see his striking profile dominated by a pronounced, Roman nose. He was a terribly skinny, elderly man, quite frail, with skin so diaphanous he appeared luminescent. Even kneeling, he seemed tall for an Italian, though his shoulders were bowed with age. Tufts of white curls sprouted out from under his white skull cap, accentuating a receding hair line and high forehead. Long, delicate, aged fingers, punctuated by the enormous blue-green emerald fisherman's ring on his right hand, were partially obscured by the lace of his sleeves as he folded his hands in prayer. His red and gold velvet slippers were barely visible beneath his vestment's ornate hem.

The old man's voice, however, defied his apparent fragility.

His clear, mellifluous baritone voice carried in the room as he prayed in Latin, "*Sancte Michael Archangele, defende nos in proelio...*"

Harden later told me that it was Leo who wrote this prayer to Saint Michael, and the fervour with which the pontiff uttered it mirrored the poignant plea of the words. Another short prayer or two followed this, then he finished with "Amen" making the Sign of the Cross. Using the acolyte's shoulder to his right as leverage, he stood. He turned to leave, then froze, his gaze locked on the golden tabernacle above the altar.

He stood still for several moments and no one in the room moved. While I could not see his whole face, he seemed to have a truly unhealthy pallor, and his slight frame wavered, unsteady. Concerned for his health, I moved to stand up. But Holmes at my right grabbed my forearm and gestured for me remain where I was. Holmes' expression was intent, his head tilted and lips parted slightly with surprise.

The acolyte to the Pope's right reached out and gingerly touched him on the arm. The old man's head suddenly snapped around to look at the youth, as if he'd forgotten where he was. I then saw what Holmes had from his much better vantage point—a thin line of moisture trailing the length of the pontiff's cheek.

"Oh," I murmured, barely audible.

Holmes put his finger to his lips.

Leo stepped from altar with his hands folded, then catching sight of Dionisio and our band, beckoned with a regal sweep of his fingers for us to follow him.

We did as he bade us, and arrived in a small room just behind the chapel in time to see the Pope's gentleman servant and one of the acolytes lifting the heavy outermost vestment over the old man's head while the other acolyte carefully folded another ornate garment. The pontiff quickly stuffed a white linen handkerchief into his shirt sleeve beneath his alb, and came forward to my friend with his hands outstretched.

"Signore Holmes," he said. He gripped both of my friend's hands tightly as he gazed up at him. He continued in Italian, and Harden translated in my ear. "It gladdens my heart to see you, my son. You look very well." His thin lips were stretched in a bright, fond smile, and I could see from his laugh lines that his was a face more accustomed to smiling than frowning.

Holmes returned the Pope's smile with one of equal affection. "I am, Holy Father," he said in French, "But are *you* well?"

Leo's smile dimmed slightly and he continued in the same language. "I am well for eighty-five years." As he spoke, he untied the golden cord that held in place his crisscrossed stole. "Why do you ask?" He continued to remove his vestments, handing them to a second acolyte at his other hand.

"You seemed unsteady just now." Holmes tilted his head in my direction. "My friend Dr. Watson was concerned. He nearly leapt to your assistance as you stood before the altar."

"This is Dr. Watson?" He turned to gaze at me with heavy-lidded dark brown eyes that sparkled with such profound warmth and sadness I was struck with awe. He gently but firmly gripped my right hand, his face wearing a loving smile. "It is a pleasure to meet you, Doctor. I have read many of your stories to keep abreast of the marvellous things our friend here is doing."

"Really?" I managed to gasp, blinking in surprise.

The old man patted my shoulder, and said tenderly, "Don't worry about me, dear son. My body is burdened by age and my spirit burdened by many other things." He glanced back at the first acolyte, who stepped forward to remove the alb over his head so that he stood before us in a plain linen shirt, his shoulders draped with a white linen cloth, and his clerical collar, and white trousers.

The pope then noticed Harden behind me. "Is this a friend with you?"

"My apologies, Holiness," Holmes said. "This is our host John Vincent Harden."

"Signore Harden, yes, our American neighbour. I've not had the pleasure." He clasped the millionaire's hand, and Harden went to his knee in Catholic fashion to kiss the Pope's fisherman's ring.

"The pleasure is all mine, Holy Father."

"*Grazie*, Signore," Leo said, patting his hand then making a cross in blessing over him. "But we should get on with our sad business—" He turned quickly to his attendants behind him. "*Presto, tutti*," he said to them. "I must go—"

The Pope's assistants hurried frantically at his command. The second acolyte removed the linen cloth from Leo's shoulders, while his middle-aged butler held up the Pope's white cassock so the pontiff could slip his arms into the sleeves. The first cleric then knelt at the pontiff's feet to fasten the silk-covered buttons from the bottom, while the butler then laid a simple gold pectoral cross around his neck.

The pontiff finished buttoning the top of his cassock and hooked the cross on the button at the centre of his chest. He then held up his arms as the butler wrapped his embroidered fringed sash around his waist, tugging it here and there to make it just so.

"*Va bene*, Pio," Leo muttered. He gently slapped his butler's hand to stop him from fussing with it. "*Basta.*" One of his acolyte's handed him a carved redwood walking stick, and with it he pointed for us precede him from the small room. "*Andiamo.*"

When we exited the room, the Pontifical Guard on each side of the door snapped to attention, with their halberds in their right hands. Dionisio quickly turned to one to say where we were heading and the soldier nodded for his fellow to precede us, while two others fell into step behind our party. It slightly unnerved me to be surrounded by soldiers carrying rather threatening Renaissance pole arms, but Leo paid them no mind. He walked with poise among them, emanating an air of imperial grace.

The departmental offices and cardinals' suites were a short walk, down the stairs to the first floor and through the Apostolic Palace. Leo walked slowly, which was understandable given his advanced age. I was impressed he did not rely much on his walking stick. At times he grew winded and slowed our pace more, but other than that he was steady. He walked between Harden and myself, politely asking us questions in

15

French about our families and our interests—wanting to learn as much as he could about his new acquaintances.

It occurred to me that while Leo XIII was surrounded by people, he had few opportunities to chat with anyone new, at least not in an informal setting. He would not leave the Vatican because of tense relations with the new government of Italy and its perceived threat to take the Vatican away or cause him harm. He was, essentially, a voluntary prisoner in a world he laboured to open to all. I therefore did my best to accommodate his desire for polite conversation, and found myself charmed by his kindly, solicitous demeanour. Occasionally, when speaking of himself in his role as pontiff, he'd use the royal "We," which I found somewhat unsettling. It reminded me that the man beside me was not merely a charming Italian gentleman—or that he most certainly did not consider himself to be.

Holmes, meanwhile, walked to my right, quiet and thoughtful. I could tell he was pondering something, so I did not draw him into the conversation, allowing him his mental solitude.

When we arrived at Cardinal Tosca's suite, His Holiness said nothing to the guards, but waved impatiently for them to open the door. One removed a set of keys from his pocket, and unlocked the suite, then stepped aside to allow us entrance.

"After you, Signore," the pontiff said, motioning for my friend to walk ahead of us into the room. Holmes nodded respectfully and strode into the room hands clasped behind his back.

"Giocomo." The pope stopped Dionisio, resting his hand on his shoulder. "Summon Brother Michele."

The young priest bowed and hurried away.

As Harden, the pope, and I were familiar with how Holmes worked, all three of us placed ourselves at outer edge of the room while he examined the grim scene, scouring it with his hawk-like gaze.

The deceased was seated near a cold fireplace, slumped over his writing desk in his black, red-trimmed cardinal's cassock, just as Dionisio had described. His hands were splayed outward on the dark wood desktop, as if he had grasped it to rise to his feet in his last moments. His skin had a bluish pallor that I attributed to asphyxiation. Holmes walked around the table, scrutinizing it and the dead man. Lifting each of the cardinal's hands, he inspected them. Holmes then touched the top of the cardinal's left hand with his index finger, then rubbed his index finger and thumb together. He then sniffed them. "Olive oil," he muttered. "Ah—he received Last Rites, Holiness?"

"Extreme Unction," Leo corrected him in a fatherly tone. "Yes, I anointed him myself." The pontiff stood in front of the window creating a thin silhouette in the sun. He was thumbing an ebony rosary in his right hand, and looked grieved at the scene before him. "I was careful, Signore. I did not want to wait—"

Holmes waved the comment away. "Do not worry, Holiness. You disturbed nothing, really." He inspected the empty pen holder at the front edge of the desk, flipped through a few papers, then opened the drawer from which he removed a much-buried fountain pen. He took up a piece of paper and scratched a few marks. He shook the pen, then allowed a drop of ink to drop onto the palm of his opposite hand. He smudged this with his thumb, then placed his palm next to the dead man's finger. "No," he whispered. "That's not it. Where is it?"

"Where's what?" I asked.

"The fountain pen."

"What fountain pen?"

"That's the point, there isn't one—at least not the correct one. Observe, Watson." He motioned for me to join him next to the corpse and lifted the man's right hand. "The ink is not the same shade. Also, he has a fresh paper cut on the end of his index finger, and when he used a fountain pen to write, it did as many fountain pens do—it leaked."

"Covering the cut."

"Precisely."

"Is that important?"

"I am not sure. I'll have to do some research."

"Researching ink and paper cuts?" Harden snorted. "Be serious, Holmes."

Holmes raised an eyebrow at the millionaire. "I am always serious about such things."

17

"You may have free access to our library here, Signore."

"Thank you, Your Holiness. That would suit me nicely. By the way—" He tapped the desktop. "Did you see a pen here when you anointed the body?"

Leo shook his head. "Only what you see there."

Holmes grunted. "There is one other thing that's puzzling me."

"What's that?"

"What was he writing? There are no papers with fresh writing on them. I wonder—"

Holmes scanned the room one more time, then turning his attention to the floor he walked slowly across the rug toward Harden who stood beside the door. At one point he crouched, running his fingers over the rug. "Scuff marks," he muttered. "Two from the heels of a lady's shoe, another one from a man's boot. There was a struggle here. How many came in here after the body was discovered, Holiness, do you know? There seems to have been some additional foot traffic on top of these marks."

"You would need to confirm it with the cardinal's secretary," Leo replied. "But I observed very few. I know of only the Captain of the Guard, the cardinal's secretary, Brother Michele, and myself. When I arrived I asked the other guardsmen to remain outside so nothing would be disturbed."

Holmes nodded. His fingers brushed over a wrinkle in the Persian rug directly in front of the millionaire's feet. "Would you step to your right, please?"

Harden did as he asked without comment and Holmes flipped back the edge of the rug. "Ah-ha!" he exclaimed and lifted a small white card from the floor.

"How did that get there?" Harden asked. "Is that writing on it?"

Holmes held the card in front of the millionaire's eyes, and smiled triumphantly.

"Rosalinda Maddio!" Harden cried. He took the card from Holmes and read it again to be sure. "How could that be?"

"You know this woman?" Holmes asked.

"I do. She is the seventeen-year old daughter of a prominent

Italian family who are close friends with my in-laws. Her parents emigrated to Britain where she was born. She is a very talented young artist—a prodigy if I might be so bold to say so. Her sculpture is magnificent. She's staying with my wife's sister here in Rome so she might be properly chaperoned while she applies to the cameo art school."

"This school accepts women?" Holmes asked. "That is unusual."

"Well, she is singular," said Harden. "They are considering her application despite her sex because of her God-given talent."

Holmes beamed. "Mr. Harden, you have just proven your worth in this case."

At that moment a red-haired, fair-skinned young man wearing a black cassock entered the room. Out-of-breath from running, he went to his knees before the pontiff and panted in Italian (which Harden translated for me), "Am I late, Holy Father? I was eating with the other seminarians. Please forgive me—"

"Brother Michele, I presume?" Holmes concluded aloud.

The youth looked in surprise at Holmes, "Yes, Signore."

"This is Signore Sherlock Holmes, Brother Michele," said Leo.

"Oh!" He rested his hand on his breastbone while he caught his breath. "It's good that you are here, Signore."

"I have a couple of questions for you, if don't mind. Why don't you sit down for a moment and rest?" Holmes pulled the chair back from the nearby breakfast table and motioned for him to sit.

The seminarian looked hesitantly at the pope, who gave him a permissive nod.

"*Grazie*, Signore," the winded youth said as he took his seat.

Holmes asked, "Were you outside the entire time the young woman was here this morning?"

Michele shook his head, "Oh no. My place is through this adjoining room. I came outside to the hall when I heard the girl weeping."

"Did you hear her cry out or any other noise?"

"No, Signore."

"And you saw the nephew with the girl in the hall."

"Yes. He was guiding the girl out. She was dragging her feet and seemed truly distraught—"

"Why do you say that?"

"Well, he seemed to be having trouble holding her up—as if she were fighting to go back to the cardinal's office. She was slumped in his arms. I asked Giuseppe what was happening and he told me his uncle had asked him to call a cab for her."

"And you took him at his word?"

"At the time I didn't see any reason not to, Signore. I suppose on second thought I could have inquired further."

Holmes' expression was grim as he turned from Michele to Dionisio who had slipped in the room to stand just inside the door. "The cardinal's nephew made no mention of knowing this young lady?"

Dionisio looked confused. "Not at all."

"I didn't get that impression either," said Michele.

Holmes turned to Harden and gestured politely for the card, which Harden returned. He held it in front of the young man's eyes. "Is this the *carte de visite* you took to His Eminence this morning?"

A relieved smile brightened Michele's face. "Yes! Where did you find it? I looked everywhere!"

"It was under the rug in front of the door. I have my own theory on how it came to be there. Did you read what she'd written on the card before you took it in?"

The youth's pale cheeks reddened. "I—"

"You don't read English."

He shook his head. "I wish I did, Signore. His Eminence knew English. He spent a year in England as a bishop advising a papal commission on the question of Anglican ordination. I assumed from her manners that the young lady would write nothing insulting, and that His Eminence would see her or not based on what she wrote."

"You have a good deal of trust."

Michele set his jaw and his grey-green eyes flashed with irritation. "Some may call it faith, Signore."

"Your faith is not in question, my son," said Leo who had moved to stand by Holmes. "There is no need to be defensive."

"I'm sorry, Holy Father, I—" He looked over at the dead cardinal across the room, then rubbed his eyes. "I just can't believe this is happening."

Holmes rested a comforting hand on the young man's shoulder and Michele relaxed slightly. "What can you tell me about the cardinal's nephew?"

"His nephew?" The seminarian raised his head and gazed at my friend quizzically.

"Yes, that is what she wrote on the card." He showed it to us. Under her name was the graceful flourish of a female hand. "'Regarding your nephew.' What can you tell me about him?"

The youth blinked, clearly mystified. "Giuseppe is a pleasant, respectful student—about my age I think. His parents are from Perugia. The cardinal's late brother was Giuseppe's father, and he was a lay missionary to Colombia in South America. He and his wife died two years ago in an accident there and Giuseppe's older brother still serves there as a priest. But I believe Giuseppe's father requested the appointment when the Holy Father was archbishop of that see."

Holmes turned to Leo, who nodded. "That's true. As archbishop I signed the approval for the cardinal's brother to go to Colombia about twenty years ago. I don't recall precisely when. I also sent diocese financial support to him—as much as I could manage while fighting Perugia's annexation by Sardinia. When he left, he took his young family with him. Giuseppe had just been born."

"So the boy was raised in Colombia."

"Yes."

"And he came to Italy to study art?" Holmes asked the seminarian

"Yes, a year ago," Michele replied. "Giuseppe applied and was accepted at the school of cameo art here in Rome. He is an accomplished sculptor. He carved that statue of Saint Anthony you see there on the mantel. He also gave his uncle a fountain pen for which he'd carved a lovely outer casing of alabaster."

"A fountain pen? Do you know where His Eminence kept it?"

"HE CARVED THAT STATUE OF SAINT ANTHONY YOU SEE
THERE ON THE MANTEL."

"It would be on his desk in the pen stand. His Eminence never used it because he didn't want to waste the ink. His nephew gave it to him to use for special occasions. But even so, His Eminence thought it was a lovely and thoughtful personal gift, so he kept it where everyone could see it." Michele went to the desk, checked the pen stand as Holmes had, then moved some papers around. "That's odd," he said finally. His eyebrows furrowed. "It should be right here."

"Do you know where the nephew resides?"

"Yes, Signore, I'll give you his address." He took up a piece of note paper and the spare fountain pen and scribbled a few lines. He then handed the paper to Holmes.

"Excellent," Holmes said. He glanced around the room once more, and said, "I think we've found all there is here, Your Holiness. I would like to—"

A burst of loud, angry voices in the hall interrupted Holmes. Led by the pontiff, we all went to the door to see what the commotion was. Just outside, a young gentleman argued vociferously with the Captain of the Guard.

His Holiness put an end to the fuss with a few sharp words that Harden did not translate, but from the inflection I surmised His Holiness demanded an explanation.

"Holy Father," the gentleman said, going quickly to one knee. He was a handsome youth, sturdy of frame and square of jaw. His sharp black eyes sparkled with irritation. "I simply want to know what's happening about my uncle. I came here earlier and the door was locked."

"You are Giuseppe Tosca?" Holmes asked.

The young man turned a hard gaze upon my friend. "Yes. Who are *you?*"

"Show respect, young man," the pope said, inclining his head to my friend. "This is Signore Sherlock Holmes who is here at my request."

At the mention of his name, young Tosca's ire faded, and he managed to smile. He rose to shake Holmes' hand. "Signore, I didn't know His Holiness had summoned you. Did you simply happen to be in Rome?"

"You might say it is Divine Providence." Holmes said. "I've

already completed my inspection of your uncle's office suite. It seems to me that funeral arrangements should be made. Perhaps Brother Michele can help you with that?"

Leo nodded in agreement. "Yes, please help him, Brother," he said to the youth who stood at his shoulder. "Confer with Father Dionisio about a proper schedule for the Requiem Mass. I'll do it of course, though it will have to be here at Saint Peter's. Is that acceptable to you, Signore Tosca?"

The young man blinked. "It would be an honour, Holy Father, but—"

Holmes raised his eyebrows. "But?"

"Do you know how my uncle died? I wasn't here. I left to take the lady outside and when I came back, the door was locked. Brother Michele said he'd died suddenly and that His Holiness had given him Extreme Unction."

"Yes," said Holmes. "You'd left to escort the young lady out. Did you know her?"

"No, Signore."

"Do you know why she came to see your uncle?"

"I have no idea."

"Was she crying when you entered the room?"

"Yes. My uncle asked me to help her get a cab."

"Where did you go after that?"

The young man averted his eyes. "I went to get something to eat."

Holmes pursed his lips. His arms were crossed. "Your uncle died of heart failure."

"Heart failure?" the young man repeated.

"Yes, that's what I determined, and Dr. Watson here confirmed it."

I had worked with Holmes long enough to follow his lead. "Absolutely," I said, through Harden's translation. "His heart simply stopped beating. And—" I opened my hands innocently. "That's all it takes, I'm afraid."

The young man looked nonplussed. "I see."

"Signore Tosca, these gentlemen are no doubt hungry for luncheon and we must see to their comfort," Leo said. "Please stay with Brother Michele to be certain your uncle is properly cared for. If anything disturbs you, please don't hesitate to send word of it."

"Yes—uh—certainly, Holy Father. Thank you."

Flanked by the Pontifical Guard, we left the way we'd come. We were silent as we walked until we scaled the stairway to papal reception rooms and apartments. Our pace was slow as demanded by the pontiff's age.

"Heart failure, Signore?" Leo asked. He arched his eyebrow at my friend.

"Holmes stretched the truth a bit, Your Holiness," I said with a grin. "Everyone dies when their heart stops."

Harden rolled his eyes. "I'm surprised he actually accepted that answer."

"I gave him an answer that pacified him," Holmes said. "He wanted to know if we knew the truth, and now he thinks we don't. But he knows exactly how the cardinal died because he killed him."

Leo stopped on the stairs and the entire entourage stopped with him. "*He's* the murderer?" he asked in a hushed tone. He looked wounded at the revelation. The Captain of the Guard, who was listening to our conversation, was also clearly concerned.

"After a fashion. He created the murder weapon. He placed it within his uncle's grasp. The problem is he didn't intend to kill his uncle. He intended to kill someone else." His grey eyes gazed pointedly at the pontiff.

Leo gripped his pectoral cross—his knuckles were white. "Why?" He whispered. "How?"

"I suspect I know the why, at least partly." He held up Miss Maddio's card once more, but showed us the back. Drawn there in black ink was a symbol.

Leo's eyes grew wide and his mouth opened slightly.

"What do you see, Holy Father?" Holmes said quietly.

The pope's mouth clamped shut. His eyebrows furrowed as his expression turned grave.

"You know," Holmes prompted. "You can say."

"Throughout these seventeen years of Our pontificate," the pontiff said, pronouncing his words with intent, "We have several times reminded the faithful of certain societies and their goals to destroy the Church. Our predecessor did as well. These warnings to the faithful are well-founded and well-documented, and yet We are mocked and ridiculed for them."

"I assure you, Holiness, everyone here holds you in the highest regard and we would never behave so abominably. Pray, tell me what you see."

Leo released a defeated sigh. "The Masonic Arc and Compass."

Holmes nodded. "That is precisely what it is. His Eminence made this mark with the missing pen. He managed to leave us a clue about his killer."

"So young Tosca is a Freemason."

"I would not be surprised if he were," said Holmes. He returned the card to his pocket. "To be honest that's probably not his only motive, but it gives us something to go on. Now, as to how the young man planned to harm you, I am not positive. I need to visit your library."

"Of course," Leo nodded. "But would you not eat something first? I've had a luncheon prepared for your visit."

Holmes shook his head. "I'm on the hunt now, Holiness. I rarely eat when there's a problem to solve."

Leo gave him a wry smile. "I should not be surprised. I am the same way." He gestured with a finger for Dionisio to lean close. "Escort Signore Holmes over to the library and help him find what he needs." The young man nodded.

"Thank you, Holiness," said Holmes. "I shan't be long. And you gentlemen," he turned to the towering Captain of the Guard beside him. "You make absolutely certain that Giuseppe Tosca doesn't come within a hundred yards of His Holiness, at least until I return. You understand?"

"Without question, Herr Holmes," the captain said. "Couldn't we simply throw him out?" The soldier looked hopefully to his master in white.

"That would be my personal preference," Leo said. "Without

a proper prison we cannot hold him here. Lord knows the Italian government has not been accommodating with incarcerating those who commit crimes on Vatican soil."

"It would make all of us feel better to simply hurl him in the Tiber," said Holmes. "But that would set him loose. No, we want him where we can watch him. Your men can handle that, no?"

The guardsman smiled. "Without question." He raised his eyebrows at the pope. "Holy Father?"

Leo gave the man an impatient wave. The captain saluted the pontiff and left to see that it was done.

Holmes turned to follow Dionisio, and we continued up the stairs into the papal residence. As we crossed the apartment threshold Leo suddenly clutched my arm. His face was tight with anxiety.

"Are you all right, Your Holiness?" I asked in French.

"My heart *is* still beating," he said with a worried frown. "In spite of all of this."

The bells of the noon Angelus tolled from St. Peter's as we entered the dining room. Leo paused at that moment to pray the required short devotion along with Harden and the several servants. I bowed my head out of respect, remembering it, though in English, from my childhood days in Anglican schools. When this was finished, he invited Harden and me to join him at the table.

The meal in the papal apartment was simple but elegantly prepared. It was Friday, so after His Holiness said a prayer of thanks in Latin, a delicate whitefish was presented to us in a white garlic butter sauce with penne pasta and green vegetables. The servants also provided fresh bread with peppered olive oil, as well as prima piatti of fresh mozzarella and tomato decorated with a sprig of basil. A bottle of dry Orvieto was appropriately chilled beside the table. I noticed that Leo didn't eat much at all. He took a few bites, and proceeded to poke at his fish thoughtfully. His slender build told me this was probably common. Then again, he no doubt mourned his fellow bishop, which would be enough to squash anyone's appetite.

He thumbed the stem of the glass, his face gaining a morose cast to it as he drifted into his thoughts.

Hoping to distract him, I politely queried him on the meaning of papal infallibility. He was quite affable about it and explained it in the most humble of terms, saying that he was merely infallible when teaching the Church on matters of faith and morals because Christ protects the Church from him, a fallible man. Strangely enough, I found it made some sense—though being un-churched, I am perpetually doubtful.

Suddenly the door burst open and Holmes entered holding a large book above his head triumphantly. "Gentlemen—Your Holiness." Holmes bowed his head with a large smile. "I've found it!" He dropped open the book on the table with such a thump the tableware rattled. Leo stood as did we all to look at the opened tome and the page Holmes had chosen.

"A frog?" I asked, befuddled.

"Not just any frog, Watson. *Phyllobates terriblis*—the yellow poison dart frog from the north coast of South America—particularly *Colombia*."

"What book is this?" asked Leo lifting the cover to peer at it.

"A comprehensive wildlife and culture journal written by a missionary to South America. Brilliantly produced in Latin I might add." He tapped the page of the book with his index finger, grinning ear-to-ear. "This frog produces a poison on its skin that is instantly deadly to humans. No doubt kin to the South American poison Jefferson Hope used to make his toxic pills of revenge from our first case together, Watson. If a drop of this poison enters an open wound or one imbibes the tiniest of drops, they die in seconds of asphyxiation."

"Good Lord," I whispered.

"So—what does this have to do with the cardinal?" Harden asked.

"Simple," said Holmes. "Our young killer poisoned the ink in the pen just as the natives of Colombia do their darts."

"The ink in the paper cut!"

"Precisely. That is why the ink consistency was different to my eyes, how I knew it was a different pen. And this poison pen provides its own wound—one that resembles a paper cut. I suspect a tiny razor slides from the side of the pen casing to nick the skin. Then it is specially designed to 'leak' like any common fountain pen may do. It's not unlike Mr. Culverton Smith's ivory box, if you'll remember, Watson, though far more artistic and effective. I am, of course, eager to examine the device.

"But here is what I believe the boy had in mind," Holmes continued. "It is a flawed plan. I don't believe he thought it through fully, though the pen is definitely a stroke of genius." Holmes flashed a quick grin, seemingly amused at his own pun.

"I believe," he continued, "That young Tosca gave the pen to his uncle and suggested His Eminence save it for a special event, such as Your Holiness visiting his office. At such an occasion, the cardinal offers you this elegant pen of carved alabaster for you to write with and you drop dead right there on the spot."

Thunderstruck, Leo's dark eyes were wide.

"As I said," Holmes continued. "The plan is flawed. The biggest flaw is, of course, that his uncle might accidentally kill himself—and that's exactly what happened. His Eminence had not wanted to use the pen, as Brother Michele said. Now, Signorina Maddio somehow encountered Tosca through their mutual interests at the school. She came to inform the cardinal of something she'd learned about him, we might assume his Masonic affiliation. While she was there in his suite, His Eminence searched for a fountain pen to write something. But he could not find the pen he wanted because it is shoved back in the drawer. He therefore took the special one from his pen stand to write, but he was immediately affected by the poison. He only had time to write one thing, so he brilliantly sums up what the girl told him with one symbol on the card he had in his hand. He died in front of her. She was, of course, horrified—"

"Wouldn't she scream, Holmes?" I asked.

"Not necessarily. Not all women scream. Some faint, some weep, some become as clams. This one apparently weeps." Holmes waved his hand as if brushing away a fly.

"In any event, young Tosca arrived, probably following her

here. He took the pen and the card to cover the evidence and struggled to take her God knows where, threatening her with instant death at the point of the pen to keep her silent. As he guided, or rather, *dragged*, the struggling girl from the room he dropped her card by the door, and he or she inadvertently kicked it under the rug—"

"Good Lord." Harden's face grew pale. "Miss Rosalinda—!"

Leo blanched as well. Tapping his right fist in his opposite hand, he turned to look out the window behind him. The rain clouds had now blotted the sun, making it seem as dusk in the early afternoon sky.

The pope turned back to us, his dark eyes flashing with decision. "Giocomo!" He commanded suddenly. "Come here."

Father Dionisio came quickly to his master's side.

"Remove your cassock."

"Holiness?"

"*Subito!*" As Leo spoke, he lifted the pectoral cross over his head and set it on the table. He then unwrapped the sash from around his waist and tossed it on his chair. "*Presto! Presto!* We have no time to waste."

Hurriedly, the young man unbuttoned his cassock even as Leo unbuttoned his own. Holmes came around the table and knelt to help Leo with the lower buttons.

"What on earth —?" I asked.

"You'll see," said Holmes.

Dionisio removed his cassock and stood in simple black shirt, clerical collar and black trousers. Holmes helped Leo slip out of his white cassock and into the black gown provided by Dionisio. The black was almost the right size, though fuller through the midsection due to Dionisio's thicker frame.

"You're not serious, Holiness," said Harden. "You're not actually *leaving* the Vatican. Someone may recognise you—"

"'If the highest aim of a captain were to preserve his ship,'" Leo replied, quoting what I later learned was Aquinas. "'He would keep it in port forever.'" He buttoned the top of the cassock while Dionisio crouched to fasten the bottom. "We must go. An innocent child is in danger for my sake."

"Signore Harden is right, Holiness," said Dionisio from floor. "This is madness."

"*Basta.*" Leo pulled young man from the ground by the elbow. He gestured emphatically with an open hand to the top of his head. "*Portami un cappello. Presto!*" Dionisio dashed into the next room. "And black stockings and shoes—ah, never mind I'll find something." The pontiff marched with remarkable energy into a side room that I guessed to be his sleeping area and returned promptly with black calf-length boots. His gentleman servant now trailed him protesting in rapid Italian as His Holiness moved. While the pontiff sat on a small bench to kick off his red slippers and pull on the boots, the agitated servant knelt beside him rambling so quickly that neither Harden nor I could decipher any meaning from him.

Apparently the meaning didn't register to Leo either. "*Basta, basta, BASTA!*" He barked, stomping his boot-covered foot. He pointed a thumb to his chest. "*Ego sum Petros!*" He made sweeping gesture to drive the man from in front of him. "*Vai!*" Struck with terror, the butler dodged from the old man's path as Leo charged to a baroque style cherry wood cabinet. From it he removed a worn, black leather case that he tucked under his arm. He finished buttoning his cuffs and Dionisio returned with a small, wide-brimmed black hat, which Leo snatched from him. He then plucked off his white zucchetto and slapped it into the bewildered priest's hands.

"*Allora*, Signori," Leo said to us, dropping the black hat on his head. "*Andiamo.*"

"You've forgotten one detail, Padre," said Holmes, in reference to the pope's new attire.

"*Che?*"

"*L'anello.*" Holmes held up his right hand and pointed to his fourth finger.

"Ah." Leo pulled the fisherman's ring from his finger and dropped it into the left pocket of the black cassock. The young priest then handed him a tall black umbrella, and Leo set its end to the floor with authoritative thud.

It is amazing how clothes can change the appearance of a man. Where once stood the proverbial Vicar of Christ on

Earth, now stood a simple, venerable Italian priest. Strangely, he resembled the aged Italian cleric persona Holmes once adopted to avoid the notice of Professor Moriarty.

I glanced at Holmes and saw him giving me a knowing grin. "Very well then," he said. "As the man says—let's go."

Harden asked, "Go *where*, though, Holmes? We have no idea where he's taken her." We filed out the door and into the hall. I noticed that the guards at the door made no movement as we left. Leo's disguise had escaped their notice.

"We'll start at his boarding house," Holmes said leading us down the stairs. "If she's not there, we'll find something that'll point us to where he took her, I'm certain of it. The young man is careless, a flaw that places him a mark below an effective criminal mind. But time is definitely of the essence."

When we reached the front door to the Apostolic Palace, the Captain of the Guard was there with the two door guards. He turned to us and when he recognised the pontiff in simple priest's attire, his mouth dropped open in alarm.

"Holy Fa—"

"Ssssst!" Leo hissed, holding up his hand.

"But—!"

"Captain, I'll take responsibility," Holmes said. "We'll protect him with our very lives. Is the young man still here?"

The stunned soldier nodded. "My lieutenant just said he was finishing up with the morticians. They won't be much longer. But—"

"Go ahead and let him leave. If you can, delay him with some questions and nice words about his uncle."

"But—!"

"Let's go, gentlemen. Quickly!" Holmes walked at a hurried stride out the palace building and through the colonnade into St. Peter's square, where pilgrims and other tourists were still milling and carriages were plentiful despite the threat of rain. The pontiff simply could not move at the pace Holmes had set, so I stayed back with him while Holmes and Harden jogged ahead to hail a cab. Even so, by the time Leo and I reached the stopped carriage, the old man was badly winded. Together Holmes and I assisted His Holiness into the carriage. When I slid into the seat next to him, the pope's eyes were closed and his hand was on his chest.

"Holiness?" I whispered.

"It's still beating, Doctor," he said, taking a gasp of air. "And with much ferocity."

"Breathe deeply—you have a few moments to rest."

"With this nose, I can't help but breathe deeply."

As the carriage started on its way, Leo reached into the pocket of the cassock and I heard several items clinking together, one of which was probably his ring. He looked up at all of us, chuckled, then coughed. "Giocomo always has so many things in his pockets," he said. "He usually has his breviary in here—thank God he took that out. Is that a pocket knife?" After some rummaging, he finally pulled out Dionisio's black rosary. He kissed the crucifix and made the sign of the cross. He then prayed silently for several minutes with his eyes closed, regulating his breathing with the movement of his beads. When he opened his eyes a slit, he seemed to realise I was still watching him, concerned. He smiled and explained, "*Per la giovine.*"

"Oh." He was praying for the young woman. "That'll help." Leo nodded and went back to his rosary.

The pontiff made his way around the set of beads by the time we'd reached the pensione boarding house where the young man was staying. I was relieved that the pope was breathing better, but I was determined to remain close to him for the rest of our adventure, lest he overexert himself.

Large rain drops began to fall as I helped His Holiness from the carriage. Holmes and Harden went to ring the bell, making room for us under the building portico. A middle aged grey-haired matron answered the door wearing a pristine, white apron.

"Good afternoon, Signora," said Holmes. "I was wondering if we might visit the rooms of Giuseppe Tosca."

"He is not here, Signori. Would you like to leave a message?" She was a plump, pleasant woman, though guarded. She studied all of us shrewdly—her eyes coming to rest upon the elderly priest at my side. "*Buon giorno*, Padre," she said with a small, respectful curtsy.

"*E lei*, Signora," Leo replied with a nod.

I could tell that we now had an ally—the clergyman added a sense of credibility to our group.

"Signora," Holmes said. "We are all here because we believe your tenant has taken a young woman against her will. Were you here all day today?"

"*Madre di Dio!*" Her hand flew to her breastbone. "No, Signore, I went out early this morning to the market and I was out until just a short time ago."

"Do you have a key to his rooms?"

"Absolutely. Please come with me."

She led us into her tidy boarding home. The main hall was decorated in Greco-Roman style and smelled of fresh baked bread and oregano. After grabbing a set of master keys from a side table, she led us to the stairs. I gestured for the pope to precede me up to Tosca's suite on the second floor, where the matron unlocked the door with trembling hands. "Here you are, Signori."

Without prompting, Holmes strode into the suite first and turned on the gas lamp even as a flash of lightning illuminated the window. The main room was a long, neat, furnished space arranged as an artist's studio. A blue and yellow Persian rug covered half the floor, and a small table and chairs were situated on the other end of the room. A table littered with carving tools, paint brushes, paint, and several small sculptures, some painted, sat next to the window to the right, and in that corner was a large armoire. Holmes opened the armoire first, and saw that it contained art supplies. A bookshelf full of books lined half the wall. Holmes glanced at these, but walked straight into the adjoining bedroom.

In this room were a bed, dresser, and a large, black leather steamer trunk sitting on end, a water closet and a large, heavy wardrobe. The floor was also covered by a Persian rug that matched the one in the outer room. Holmes stood in the middle of the room, staring at the carpet, while I went to the steam trunk.

"Do you want to examine the trunk, Holmes?"

"No. That trunk has not been opened recently." He went across the room to the closet.

"How do you know?"

"The rug, Watson. Opening the trunk would scrape across it and leave a mark."

He attempted to open the wardrobe, but the door was locked. "Do you have a key for this?" he asked the woman.

She nodded and presented a skeleton key. When she unlocked it, Holmes flung it open and inside was an unconscious young woman in an emerald green walking gown, gagged and bound hand and foot. Folded in half like a rag doll, her long, honey brown hair was a curly mop, covering her face and shoulders.

"*Dio mio!*" the old matron cried.

Harden helped me lift her limp body from the wardrobe and we carried her to the bed. "Tell the matron to get brandy," I said to Harden. "And a glass of cool water."

Hearing Harden's orders in Italian, the woman nodded and rushed to get the items I requested.

Leo came alongside me and asked in French. "Is she well?"

I took the balled up rag from the girl's mouth and felt for her pulse. "She needs air and water, but yes, your prayers have been answered. You have that pocket-knife?"

Eager to help, Leo set aside his umbrella and dug Dionisio's knife from the deep pocket of his cassock. I cut loose Rosalinda's bonds while Harden propped her head with a pillow. I brushed hair from her face and I realised that she was quite lovely.

"It's a relief that we don't need that," Harden said, indicating the case under the pontiff's arm.

"No, no anointing tonight," Leo said. "Thank the Lord."

The matron returned with the brandy and the water.

"Signora," Holmes said. "Please, go downstairs and watch for Tosca. If you see him coming, warn us."

"Absolutely, Signore."

After the old woman left, I poured a bit of the brandy into

her lips. She woke with a start, coughed, and pushed my hand away. When her large green eyes opened, she sat up slowly.

"Who—? Where—?" She then squinted at the man next to me and said, "Mr. Harden?"

"I'm relieved to see you, Miss Rosalinda," he replied. "Do you feel all right?"

"What are you —? Oh no, I'm still *here!*" She jumped up from the bed, but her legs didn't cooperate and she rocked shakily. "Oh my head."

"Sit down," I said helping her back onto the bed. I handed her the water. "Sip this slowly."

She did as I ordered, then asked, "Who are you?"

"I'm Dr. Watson and this other gentleman is Mr. Sherlock Holmes."

She sputtered and coughed on inhaled water. Gazing up at my friend, she let go a nervous choked laugh. "Oh no, please. He's not Sherlock Holmes."

"Indeed I am," said Holmes.

"You can't be. You're too handsome."

Leo chuckled. Holmes, meanwhile, blushed. His lips pressed together in uncomfortable frown.

"I've read some of Dr. Watson's stories and I've seen some portraits. You definitely do look like Watson," she said to me. "Broad shouldered and sweet. But you don't look like Holmes," she said to my friend. "Well, maybe a bit. Just—more handsome than I pictured." Miss Maddio then turned to the pontiff. "And you, Padre—you look just like the pope!"

"Really?" Leo's smile was bright. "But if you don't know what Signore Holmes looks like, how would you know the face of His Holiness?"

"I have his photograph from a couple years ago on a prayer card. I used it to carve a relief in sardonyx for my portfolio. He has an interesting face—cute as a little bug."

"You hear this, Holmes?" Leo said, elbowing him gently in the ribs. "You are too handsome, and I am as a *bug*. How positively charming." He gave the young lady a playful wink.

The colour completely drained from Miss Maddio's face.

"Oh my — " she clapped her hand over her mouth. "It is *you!*" She slipped from the bed to her knees. "I'm so sorry, Holy Father, please forgive me—"

"Oh, no," Leo said. He took one of her arms and I took the other to help her back onto the bed. "Child, you were bound, gagged and locked up all day. There is no need for ceremony right now."

"Nor," said Holmes, impatiently, "is there *time* for it."

But Miss Maddioi was clearly overwrought. This was, no doubt, the unexpected climax to her truly terrible day. She choked out a sob. "I'm so sorry. It's really you and I'm so rude. My head is uncovered in your presence!"

"Oh, dear, Signorina— please don't." Troubled by her emotional display, Leo pulled his handkerchief from his shirt cuff and placed it in her trembling hands, then removed the hat from his own head and placed it on hers. "There. Don't cry, daughter. Everything's all right. See?"

"Signori!" The matron of the house called as she ran up the stairs. "He's coming up the street!"

"This interview will have to continue later." Holmes waved for me to help the girl up, and he led the way out into the studio. "Signora," Holmes said to the matron in the hall, "take the young lady into that other suite across the hall with you and lock the door." He turned to Leo. "You should go with them."

The pontiff straightened indignantly. "Signore, I may be old, but I am a man, not a mouse. I'll not hide away with the women."

Holmes sighed. "No, Holy Father, you're more the lion as your name implies. But if you'd please stand over in that corner by the bedroom door so you're not immediately visible as he enters, it would put me more at ease."

"*Va bene.*" He took a spot in the shadowy corner Holmes indicated.

"And you two," he said to Harden and me. "Stand on either side of the door. If he tries anything, bring him down."

I was accustomed to Holmes setting the stage for a dramatic confrontation. And I was used to altercations as a former soldier. But at times I wondered if Holmes ever considered my old

Afghan war injury in his plans when he wanted me to tackle someone.

I sighed and did as he requested, knowing I was probably in for some pain.

After locking the door, Holmes took a cigarette from his cigarette case, lit it in the lamp, and then turned off the gas. In the shadows, he then leaned his lanky frame against the art table facing the villain's entrance. The glowing ember of his cigarette pinpointed his location. Only the momentary flash of lightning revealed his form. In the silence, the sound of the rain pattered upon the roof, interrupted only by the low rumble of thunder.

A moment or two later we heard footsteps on the stairs then a key in the lock. The door opened and Tosca entered, turning up the light. He was dipping wet and visibly surprised to see Holmes, who puffed some smoke casually and said, "Signore Tosca, it's good to see you."

Harden closed the door behind him and leaned against it. Tosca turned to look at the two of us blocking his exit, then back to Holmes. "I suppose Signora Lucci let you in."

Holmes turned the chair by the art table out and offered it to Tosca. "If I may reverse the roles of host and guest, I invite you to be seated."

Straightening his damp jacket with an indignant air, Tosca did as Holmes requested. He did not seem all that concerned. "Let me guess." He crossed his arms. "You're going to explain, to the amazement of your friends, how I did the deed?"

"I've already told them that. It would be old news. They also know that you blundered badly." The pride on the artist's face turned to annoyance. "What we simply want to know is *why*."

Ego bruised, Tosca seethed for a moment before answering. "I want it gone."

"What?"

"The Church."

"Why?"

"It destroyed my family and it holds the world hostage to its archaic philosophies. The rest of Italy and even the world are finally seeing its uselessness, its pride, its stupidity. It's best that it be wiped from the earth."

I winced at these words, knowing the pope was hearing them. To his credit, he remained silent in his hiding place, allowing the young man to go on.

"I joined the Masons because I share their views," Tosca continued. "I made the Quirinal government aware of my connections and allegiance and they gave me their blessing to use it to their advantage."

Holmes grunted. "So how did the Church 'destroy your family,' as you say? Seems to me you're doing a fine job of that yourself."

Another needle pricked the young man's pride. Tosca's eyes became as slits. "My parents raised me in Colombia. Do you know what a bedlam that place is?"

"Enlighten me."

"It is uncivilised. Jungle and insects and frogs. Poor beggar Indians who cannot provide for themselves, who come to you with open hands and open mouths in the steaming, stinking heat. My father laboured for years with these ingrates, giving all his time to them and ignoring his family. And what did he have to show for it? He and my mother are killed in the night with a dart gun. My older brother, not wanting my father's dream to die, became a priest and continues to serve there. But I was smart. I left."

"And you blame all this on the Church?"

"It sent us there."

"From what I understand, your father wanted to go there himself and asked for permission."

"Inspired by false piety to an imaginary god of false principles!" Tosca pointed his thumb to his chest. "Man can think for himself. He doesn't need a dried up old man in white robes with the delusions of kingship telling him how to live his life." Tosca's dark eyes suddenly locked on the man in the corner. "Speak of the *devil*." A sinister, cruel smile crossed the young man's lips. "*Your Holiness*, I am honoured that you'd bless my humble quarters with your august presence. I'm surprised that you'd find me important enough to leave the velvet security of the Apostolic Palace."

Leo took two steps into the light. His wiry body was vibrating with fury. "We didn't come here for *you*," he said crisply. "We came for the young lady."

"'*We.*'" Tosca snickered. "You hear this? '*We!*' How terribly sad. He still clamours for the kingdom Italy's rightfully taken from him. He's so delusional he doesn't believe she'll never return it. Pathetic." He shook his head. "Now where were we? Yes, the lady. Lovely isn't she? I met her only this morning, you know. She had the misfortune to overhear a conversation of mine at school with a Masonic brother in the Quirinal. She was chaperoned, of course. But I followed her to her home to see if she would do something about what she'd heard, and sure enough, a few moments later she slipped out and hailed a cab to the Vatican. I was surprised she knew who I was but—how could she not? My work is brilliant."

"Not a bit conceited are you?" Harden remarked.

"Mock me all you want," Tosca returned. "But there is nothing any of you can do about this. The Quirinal protects me. They are the law in Italy now and I am their trusted agent. And they couldn't care less about a dead cardinal in the Vatican. In fact, they're probably rejoicing right now."

"What about kidnapping a young woman with intent to murder?" Harden asked.

Tosca rolled his eyes. "I wasn't going to kill her."

"What were you going to do with her, then?" Holmes asked.

For a moment the young man's confident expression withered. "I—wasn't sure."

"You weren't *sure?*" Holmes repeated. He blew out some smoke. His dark eyebrows furrowed in an irritated expression. "Did you not have a *plan*, boy?"

"I don't know. She's a fellow artist and pretty, I didn't want to—"

"You couldn't face her, you mean," Holmes said. "You could commit murder when you didn't have to be there to see it happen, but when it came to looking into the lovely face of your victim you had no nerve."

"No—I don't know—I—didn't know what to do with her. I didn't plan for her to be there. I just didn't want her sounding an alarm."

"You better not have touched her improperly." Harden growled.

"I had to touch her to get her here." A sudden slight smile crossed Tosca's face, "I'll admit, some of it was pleasurable, but—"

"You should not have touched her at all," Leo said sternly. "And to lust after her in such a fashion is scandalous."

Tosca leaned forward in his chair. "Old man, I have a healthy interest in women. You probably wouldn't understand that because you're just a scrawny old peacock in a dress."

"That's it." Harden snarled. He started to remove his coat. "I'm going to take his head off."

"Be at peace, Signore Harden," Leo said calmly, holding up his hand to the brawny gentleman. As he spoke, his cheeks were flushed and his thin shoulders trembled. "Our Lord suffered greater insults than to be called a peacock. If He can endure being scourged and mocked, I can suffer something as trivial as that."

Holmes said, "Signore Tosca, I think you'd better be more concerned with your welfare." He extinguished his cigarette in a paint tray on the art table. "You see, in addition to your first blunder, your second is far worse and will cause you to rot in prison at the very least."

"What are you talking about?"

"Simply that Signorina Maddio is a subject of Her Brittanic Majesty."

Tosca tensed, surprised.

"You're not the only one with government connections, Tosca. And mine are far higher than yours. Her Majesty Queen Victoria will not allow your government to ignore a crime committed against one of her subjects—particularly an innocent young lady of refinement. And when she learns that the kidnapping is related to a cold-blooded murder that the Quirinal blessed—in the Vatican itself—and that I am the one who discovered the facts of this case—Italy will be embarrassed before the entire world. Trust me, young man, your 'brothers' in the Italian government will drop you like hot coal when word comes out. They'll let you hang."

Lightning flashed in the window, brightening the room for fraction of a second in a blue glow. Tosca was silent, his lips bent downward in a scowl. He was glaring, not at Holmes, but at Leo. The pontiff met his gaze, unwavering. But in Leo's face was another emotion that Tosca read plainly.

"Don't you pity me, old man. I'll have none of it."

The pope said nothing. He reached into his left pocket and removed something I couldn't see—grasping it in his palm.

"Why don't you say something, you pompous relic?" Tosca prompted. "You think I'm not worthy to be in your noble presence. I should get down on my knees and kiss your royal slipper. That's it, isn't it? Don't you know you approved my father's mission to Colombia? Don't you realise that you made me what I am?"

Leo sighed sadly. He took the object, his fisherman's ring, and slid it on the fourth finger of his right hand. "We think," he said in an even tone, "that you should repent of your grave sins, Giuseppe Tosca."

"Repent, you mediaeval fossil?! You're not serious!"

"Apostasy, blasphemy, murder, lust, pride—my dear son, these offences to God are serious indeed."

Tosca sneered. "I do not care."

"On the contrary, the fact that you did not want to harm the young lady is proof that you do indeed care. Your soul is not truly lost. Soften your heart and receive your Lord's forgiveness."

"Keep your forgiveness, you superstitious, old fool. I have no Lord."

Leo dropped his chin sadly. "Giuseppe, through your acts and associations you have excommunicated yourself from Christ's Church, an excommunication I cannot lift without your repentance." Thunder rumbled in the distance and the sound of falling rain in the silence of the room was like a ghostly chill. "There is little I can do, other than plead with you to reconsider—"

42

Tosca burst out laughing. He slapped his knee. "*You* plead with *me?* How absolutely *priceless!* Don't waste your breath, old man. Just make that excommunication official and write me a nice, long bull like Luther's. I'd like to have it framed!"

"Young man," Leo said, his eyes misting. "It would not be worth the ink."

Instant fury twisted Tosca's features. With a scream of rage, he leaped from his chair and lunged at a very startled Leo, brandishing the alabaster pen.

"Watson!" cried Holmes.

But Harden was quicker than I. With what I later learned was a perfect American football manoeuvre (quite similar to that of rugby), he plunged his shoulder into Tosca's rib cage, sending him flying across the room. Tosca hit the floor, rolled, then began to gasp for air, his head and neck turning purple for lack of air.

Leo, meanwhile, had back-pedalled, stumbled against the table and fell hard to the floor. I ran to the old man's side as Tosca's form in the middle of the floor contorted, convulsed, then lay still.

Holmes crouched next to Tosca and turned him over—the poisonous pen had penetrated his chest through his shirt. "Amazing," Holmes murmured. Lifting the pen carefully in a folded handkerchief, he examined it. "It is almost instantaneous!"

"No," Leo groaned, his expression pained. He crawled to the young man's body. "Oh, no—no." Clenching his fist he tapped his forehead in grief.

"Holiness," I said. "It's all right—"

"No, you don't understand," he croaked, resting his hand on Tosca's chest. "This young man's soul is in Hell."

"If so, he sent himself there," said Holmes. He stood and went to the art table. Picking up a spattered, black enamel paint brush case, he emptied it of its contents and placed the pen inside with the handkerchief, snapping it closed. "You heard him. He wanted nothing of repentance and rejected it. He was already lost." Holmes slipped the case into his breast pocket.

Leo only shook his head, his thin face drawn with woe.

"Here, Holiness, let us help you up." I gestured to Harden and we lifted the old man under his arms. Suddenly Leo cried out and sucked in air though his teeth.

"My ankle," he said.

"Help him to the chair," I said. Once he was sitting, I bent down to look at his booted left foot. Through the leather I could see it was already swelling.

"Are you badly hurt, Holy Father?" Holmes asked over my shoulder. His usually impassive expression was exchanged for one of genuine concern. I could see that he cared much for the old man.

"These brittle old bones," Leo muttered. "The boots are not mine, they're my chamberlain's. They're too big. That's why I tripped."

"His ankle isn't broken is it, Watson?"

"Well, the ankle may not be broken, Holmes, it may just be a sprain. I'll never get the boot off to check without cutting it off. It's best to wrap it up over the boot until we can get him home. We can cut it off there. Let's see if we can find something here I can use as a sturdy bandage."

Signora Lucci provided some spare heavy drapery fabric which served well to wrap the ankle and hold it in place. As I worked, Holmes told the matron to contact authorities about the body and gave her his information at Harden's address for them to contact him with questions. She was upset, but relieved that it was all over. She also apparently did not know that the old priest was the pope—Miss Maddio had sensibly decided to keep that secret to herself. We did not enlighten her.

As Holmes and I helped Leo stand and hop to the door, he looked back at Tosca's body with a doleful expression. Tucking his case tightly under his arm, he turned and continued, with our help, down the stairs.

There would indeed be no anointing that day.

In the cab, Miss Maddio sat between the pontiff and me facing Holmes and Harden. She still wore the hat Leo had placed on her head. Leo, meanwhile, prayed his rosary, gazing out the window into the rain. His countenance was one of gloom.

"Holmes," I said, breaking the tense silence. "You have not explained how you came to know it was Tosca who brought about his uncle's end."

"I should think it would be obvious," Holmes replied.

"Not to me," said Harden. "You just seemed to pull the answer out of thin air."

Holmes sighed. "It all revolves around the missing pen," he said. "As you'll recall, the ink on His Eminence's finger was a different kind than that of the one remaining fountain pen. Therefore, he'd used another pen, one that was not there. And since it was not there, it must have been taken by the culprit. But why would he take a pen? It had to be that it revealed the culprit's identity, or it was the murder weapon itself. I suspected it was the former until we heard that the nephew had gifted it to his uncle with a specific purpose in mind. At that point I was certain it was both.

"I knew almost immediately that Miss Maddio was not the killer, since she did not attempt to hide her identity from the secretary. Had he been a seasoned secretary and not a seminarian, he would have remembered her name, and a cold-blooded murderer would not have taken that chance. No, she came to warn him of something scandalous, as the guards said. Upon finding her *carte de visite*, it became clear the reason for her call. Add this to the young man's strange entrance and exit, the signs of a struggle, Rosalinda's reaction to him as he left with her, and the missing pen, and you have your murderer. I wasn't entirely certain how the pen killed His Eminence because I didn't have it, but I knew it had to be a virulent poison to work so quickly. On a hunch, I researched specific poisons attributed to Colombia in South America from which he'd come, and I discovered the dart frog venom."

"Bravo, Signore." Leo said. "As the Angelic Doctor once wrote, 'Reason in man is rather like God in the world.' You have proven that today."

"*Grazie*, Holy Father."

"I really must thank you, Mr. Holmes, for finding me," Miss

45

Maddio said. "And you are correct about what happened. His Eminence was very kind to see me. After he heard me out, he sat at his desk to write a note to the school's headmaster, asking him to suspend his nephew until he could investigate the matter."

"He believed you."

"He seemed to. But when he sat down to write, he picked up the pen and—it was so horrible, I cannot bear to think of it." She dropped her face in her hands. "I don't know if I can ever forget it."

"You poor child," Leo murmured. "One like you should not see such things."

"What's even more terrible is what Giuseppe did when he arrived. He checked the cardinal's body to make sure he was dead as if he simply did not care. He stuffed my card in his pocket and made me go with him, threatening me with that horrible pen. While I struggled with him, I noticed my card was sticking out of his pocket so I plucked it out in our struggle and dropped it on the floor—"

"*You* dropped the card?" Holmes asked.

"Yes, I hoped someone would find it."

A smile spread across Holmes face. "That was clever. You saved your own life."

"Yes, well, I hoped to. It didn't seem like it at the time. He had me so frightened. He said this whole thing was my fault."

Leo groaned and wiped his hand over his face.

"But it *is* my fault, don't you see? If I had minded my own business, His Eminence would be alive right now."

"Daughter, listen to me," the pope said, taking her hand. "God takes everyone in their own time. This was His Eminence's time and his death is his nephew's fault, not yours. You mustn't blame yourself for this."

Her eyes glistened. "Giuseppe was so rough with me." She shook her head with disbelief. "I've never been treated that way by a man before. He was no gentleman."

"That much was abundantly clear," Holmes remarked.

"Thank the Merciful Saviour you are unharmed," said Leo. He patted her hand, which was tight in his. "All men are not like him, Signorina. But perhaps you'll think twice before you venture off again without a chaperone."

"You'll have no argument from me, Holy Father. When I was in that wardrobe I told myself if I survived I'd become a nun!"

The old man laughed. Rosalinda looked at him, befuddled. "Signorina," he explained, gently. "One shouldn't join the convent because she fears men. She should do so because she is called by God to serve him that way. I encountered a young girl like you who brazenly wept on my feet at a public audience to enter Carmel at age fifteen, such was her call from God. But I suspect that is not the case with you." He raised his eyebrows at her.

She sighed and her shoulders sagged. "No, it's not."

"*Va bene.* There are many good gentlemen in the world. In fact, there are some in this carriage, are there not?" This was an intended jab at Holmes; Leo grinned at him.

Colour appeared in Holmes' cheeks and he looked away. But I detected a flicker of a smile at the edge of his lips.

The carriage then stopped at Miss Maddio's residence. Harden borrowed Leo's umbrella and stepped from the cab to walk the girl to her door. Before she left the carriage, Leo said, "I will need my hat, child."

"Oh!" she took it from her head and placed it in his hands. "I'm sorry, Holy Father. And thank you. You shouldn't have left the Vatican for me."

"We are a shepherd," he said with a gentle smile. "A shepherd goes to find his one lost sheep—especially one that is in danger because of Us."

"Oh, I almost forgot! Your handkerchief—" She held it out to him.

"Keep it," he said, patting her hand. "We will see each other again, for I do wish to see your art." He made the sign of the cross in blessing over her, and she left with Harden.

Once the millionaire returned, we returned Leo to the Vatican, much to the relief (and continued ire) of the Captain of the Guard. Seeing the pope's injured limb, he looked quite irritable, but helped us carry him up the stairs to the medical suite in his apartments. There I cut the boot from his foot and after a thorough examination told the weary pontiff that it was a bad sprain. By the time Leo's personal physician arrived, I'd already wrapped the ankle properly and instructed the pope's associates to apply cold, moist compresses and to keep it elevated to reduce the swelling.

"Holy Father," said Holmes, as I finished my work. "I really must offer my apologies for your injury—"

The pontiff waved away his words. "This is my own fault, my son. I knew when I put on the black cassock what it might mean. Besides, from our last meeting I should know to expect some excitement when you are near, no?" He winked at my friend. "I will offer my discomfort for the souls in Purgatory."

Leo summoned Dionisio to his side. "Giocomo, please inform our coachman that he is to take these gentlemen to Mr. Harden's villa. Unless, of course, our friends would like to stay for dinner?"

"As enticing as your invitation is, Your Holiness," I said. "I think its best we let you get some rest."

Harden nodded in agreement. "And I should return home to my wife. No doubt she's pacing the floor with worry about now."

"Ah, *va bene*. You go, then. We'll see each other soon. I hope you'll accept Our invitation to return so We might thank you properly."

"We'd be happy to, Holiness," said Holmes. Leo raised his hand in benediction to us, and we made our exit.

The invitation did arrive by private courier several days later, as promised. Harden engaged his large coach to take us, along with his wife and two-year old son, to the Vatican. We stopped along the way to take along Miss Maddio and Harden's sister-in-law, who had received invitations to the same meeting. It was a private audience held in the pope's third floor living quarters rather than in his receiving rooms where most formal audiences were held—probably due to his injury. The women were dressed in black gowns and properly veiled in black mantillas. I had to keep reminding myself that Miss Maddio was twenty-six years my junior and that I had no business admiring her. She was indeed a vision.

At the audience, Miss Maddio showed the pontiff her art portfolio, which was indeed impressive. Leo then gave all of us personal gifts. To me he presented a hand-painted Byzantine icon of St. Raphael the Archangel, which I knew would go well in my examining room, and Holmes received a matching icon of St. Michael that he later hung in our sitting room above his desk. The pope then gave us an apostolic blessing, and we left his presence. Holmes would receive a generous compensation from His Holiness when we returned home.

However, as we were leaving the papal apartments, Holmes muttered, "Blast."

"What?"

"I was going to ask him something."

"Go back," I said, taking his gift. "I'll wait."

Holmes went back quickly and knelt on one knee beside Leo's chair so they could speak at a close distance. As the two of them conversed, I saw the pontiff's face cloud with apprehension. I turned away and proceeded out into the hall. Holmes joined me a few moments later, and we continued on our way out to Harden's carriage. He was silent as we walked; his face was drawn with concern.

"Are you all right, Holmes?" I asked, finally.

"Fine, just fine," he muttered. I could tell he didn't want to discuss it, so I let him be.

The rest of our visit, Holmes was pleasant and even happy at times. But now and again I'd see him lost in thought, and the dark cloud would return.

Finally on our return trip via the private train, I saw he was drifting into those dark thoughts again, so I finally asked, "Holmes, ever since your private conversation with the pope, you've been moping. May I ask what on earth you discussed?"

"Not moping, Watson, just thinking."

"About what?"

Holmes released a puff of his clay pipe, and gazed at me thoughtfully. "Well, he pointed out that the cornerstone for the new Catholic Cathedral in Westminster would be laid on the

49

twenty-ninth. He hoped I would return to London in time to attend. I am rather glad we'll be back in time to fulfil his request."

"That's it?"

"No." Holmes set aside the book that was in his lap and took another draw on his pipe. "After I met him the first time, I stumbled across a disturbing story in the newspaper. It was hidden in the strange occurrences section—one of my favourite portions of the paper to read as you know. The story claimed that His Holiness was a visionary."

"In terms of his social theories, he is, isn't he? His encyclical on the conditions of the working class is a masterpiece."

"I do not mean that sort of visionary. I mean that he had visions."

I hesitated before I replied. "You mean—he was delusional?"

"Did he strike you as delusional, Watson? No. They claimed he had visions from God."

I blinked. "That is…unusual."

"I thought so, too. The story in question said that in 1884, while he was finishing Mass, His Holiness collapsed into what they refer to as 'ecstasy.' While in this state, he heard the voices of Christ and Satan speaking to one another. Satan proudly declared he would destroy the Church and Christ allowed him one hundred years to try. His Holiness then saw the evil spirits, demons if you will, preying upon the Church with the fruits of their corruption, and the triumphant Michael and his legions, fighting to keep them at bay. That night, he composed his prayer to Saint Michael and ordered it to be said at the end of every Mass to stave off the evil one's attack."

"That sounds rather dramatic. There are those, reading that, who might question his sanity."

"Some might, no doubt." Holmes nodded. "However, my own personal experience with him has been, and you will no doubt concur, that he is a profoundly rational man. The story seemed perhaps a bit exaggerated to me. And yet—" Holmes looked over at me, and lowered his voice. "—in his private chapel, Watson—you could not see from where you were but I could see his face plainly. When he stopped in front of the

50

tabernacle that time I am certain he saw something. I could see his expression change and his eyes following movement. I was as shocked as you probably are now. But I know that he was watching something—something was unfolding before his eyes and it brought him to tears."

A chill travelled my spine. "And you asked him what he saw?"

"I told him I believed he'd seen something unusual in the chapel, and that I was concerned."

"What did he say?"

Holmes shook his head. "He merely winked and said, *'fides credere quod nondum vides; cuius fidei merces est videre quod credis.'"* Holmes tilted his head into a thoughtful pose. "I like him, Watson, very much. He enjoys putting me on the spot as you see, but only because he is genuinely pious. He is also imperious, but in a most endearing way."

"Yes, well." I smiled. "I'm used to that."

---

*Faith is to believe what you do not see; the reward of this faith is to see what you believe.—St. Augustine, *Sermones* 4.1.1

The Vatican Cameos

"...I was exceedingly preoccupied by that little affair of the Vatican cameos, and in my anxiety to oblige the Pope I lost touch with several interesting English cases."

— Sherlock Holmes,
The Hound of the Baskervilles

INTROIT

IT WAS NOT UNTIL after I accompanied Holmes on the matter of Cardinal Tosca's murder in Rome that I paid any consideration to chronicling the first problem he'd solved for Pope Leo XIII seven years earlier. In the intervening years I'd put the idea of the previous case aside for it brought to my mind some tragic memories of those days as well as deep regret that I could not do more for a friend who had done once so much for me.

On that morning, I'd left my practice early and stopped by Baker Street to gather some fresh clothes and my shaving kit before proceeding to a patient's home on an urgent call. A sweet mother to four children was giving birth to her fifth and the delivery looked to be a very troublesome one. It would be a long night, or perhaps even days, before I returned again to our lodgings. With a heavy heart and mind I dreaded what was to come, fearing the loss of my patient, her child, or both.

Fraught with anxiety, I climbed the steps to our rooms. As I reached the landing, the door to our sitting room opened and my friend's head appeared in the hall. "Watson, how good to—" He stopped when he took in my expression. "Are you all right?"

"I am fine."

It was clear to him that I was indeed *not* fine.

"I have a rather important case that the Prime Minister passed on to me via the Foreign Office." He held up a letter on official-looking stationary. "I was hoping you might want to accompany me to the Vatican to solve a bit of trouble for His Holiness, the Pope. We'd need to pack quickly to have time to visit Scotland Yard and catch the train to Dover out of Charing Cross." He hesitated. "But I fear you are presently engaged."

"I am." I said. "I must deliver a baby to Genevieve Murray. The child is likely breech, and could very well be lost along with the mother."

"Murray? That wouldn't be—"

"The wife of Alexander Murray, the man who saved my life at Maiwand. I hope you'll excuse me if this time my work takes precedence over yours." With that, I turned on my toe and marched upstairs to my room.

"Watson." My friend called after me.

My hands trembled as I threw my medical bag and umbrella on the bed. I flung open my wardrobe, and removed a leather satchel, along with a fresh shirt, collar, undergarments, trousers, and socks.

Holmes entered my room and closed the door quietly behind him. "Watson." He rested his hand on my shoulder. "You are a fine physician. You'll do the very best you can, all that can be done, and the rest will be in the hands—"

"'—Of God,' that's what you're going to say, isn't it?" I turned to look at him. "Why do we say that, Holmes? Neither you nor I are men of faith, and yet we still say such things." Seeing the troubled expression on his gaunt features, I sighed. "She's a good woman, Holmes. A devout one. I don't know what Murray would do without her. He says she attends her Mass every morning—*every morning*, can you believe it? That is when she's not in childbed, of course. Neither you nor I have darkened the door of a church in how long? I try to minister to someone like her, wondering if perhaps she should minister to me." I sighed deeply, my emotions dissipating. "So you're off to the pope in Rome, then?"

"It would appear so."

"Well, then, deliver a request to the man from me."

"What's that?"

"Ask him to pray for her. To us it means little, but if she knows her pope is praying on her behalf, it may give her spirit enough to survive this."

"He'll receive the request directly from my lips, my friend. You can assure her of it."

"Thank you." I took up my satchel, along with my medical bag and umbrella. "Have a pleasant journey and good luck." Holmes stepped ahead of me to open the door. "And give my best to His Holiness."

"I shall."

And that was the last Holmes and I really spoke of the first problem at the Vatican. True to his word, Holmes did pass along my request to His Holiness, and sent me a telegram from the Vatican confirming it. I gave the telegram to the Murrays who appreciated Holmes' thoughtfulness. Mrs. Murray, meanwhile, did survive her ordeal, though her child, a boy, did not. He died within an hour of birth, and was baptised there in his mother's sickroom by a Roman priest as he took his last breaths. They named him John.

"Dr. Watson," the poor woman said, clasping my hand. She smiled at me despite her own pain and grief. "I know this saddens you terribly. Please do not let it weigh too heavily upon you, for I know you did all you could. Understand that now we have our very own little saint in heaven to pray for us."

Her strength of faith in such loss shamed me. Needless to say, I wanted to recall none of this for some time. But after meeting the venerable pontiff myself seven years later, I grew curious about what happened on my friend's initial trip to Rome while I was so arduously engaged. I therefore asked Holmes if he recalled the case enough to tell me about it.

Holmes went to his reference volumes, and showed me his own notes on the case which were sketchy to say the least. I therefore asked him if he would be willing to write about the situation, as it was not one without some interest. He, of course, scoffed at the idea.

"Watson, I am incapable of spinning a tale in the way you do. The narrative would read like a scientific treatise. No one wants to read about His Holiness' case in such form."

He was, sadly, correct. I had one last hope, though. By this time, now the middle of August of 1895, Holmes had received a letter from His Holiness, in which he had included a page to me. Writing a reply to him in French, I asked the pontiff what he recalled of the cameos incident, for I did very much want to chronicle it along with his most recent case with my friend.

My answer came two weeks later on a cloudy early September afternoon in the person of a timid young clergyman at our doorstep. He was sent, it seems, at the behest of the Archbishop of Westminster bearing a large brown envelope to be delivered in person to me. Mrs. Hudson led him into our sitting room just as I was sitting down to tea by myself, for Holmes had gone off on a business errand. Wearing a long, black buttoned cassock and short-brimmed black hat, the clergyman was a diminutive, callow youth with a cherubic countenance and large bright grey eyes glinting from behind thin wire spectacles. In the hand that did not hold the envelope, he clutched a black umbrella too tightly as if it were to serve him as a life preserver. Sensing this was a manifestation of his shyness, I immediately had sympathy for him.

I stood from my table and offered him my hand, "Good afternoon, Father—"

"Deacon," he said, setting his umbrella against his leg to shake my hand. "Brown, sir. I'll be ordained to the priesthood in May."

"Yes, well congratulations in advance Deacon Brown. I understand you have something for me?"

The clergyman's umbrella dropped to the floor. He moved to pick it up, but I reached it first. "Let's set this over here." I strode across the room and placed it in the umbrella stand next to the door. "Would you have some tea?"

A relieved smile curled upon his features. "That would be wonderful, Doctor, thank you." Removing his hat and setting it aside on the ottoman, he took a seat at the table as I did myself.

"Let me open that package while you pour." He handed the

envelope across, and I turned it over. The closure was secured with red wax, after the fashion of legal or state documents, and impressed with the seal, as I could make out, of Leo XIII. I smiled up at him. "You do know whom this is from, don't you?"

He nodded, lifting the teapot and pouring out for both of us. "I am mystified, however, as to why His Holiness would send Cardinal Vaughn a package to be hand-delivered to a London doctor—oh—*wait.*" A thought had dawned at him and he gaped at me. He set the teapot down with a hard *clink*. "You're Dr. *Watson*," he said. "*The* Dr. Watson—who writes of Sherlock Holmes!"

"Well, yes, young man. You didn't know that when you were sent here?"

"His Eminence said nothing and Watson is a name nearly as common as my own." He shook his head. "I simply didn't make the connection. I confess my mind has been so embroiled in a paper I must complete on Aristotle for next week that I didn't even realise—" He looked all around him. "Heavens, Mr. Holmes lives here!"

"He does indeed."

"Sir, I've read every one of your accounts of Mr. Holmes' work. I'm an admirer of what he does. His achievements in criminology inspired me to compose my graduate thesis on the role of habitual sin in the criminal mind."

"You don't say."

"And here I was wondering why on earth His Eminence summoned me to deliver this envelope. He knows my thesis topic, and actually seemed to be discouraging it. And now—" He shook his head and smiled. "Sir, you don't know what this means to me."

"I think I do, Deacon," I said, smiling at the wisdom of the cardinal sending this particular young man on this errand. "Let's find out what's in the envelope, shall we?" After slicing under the seal with a butter knife, I slid the pages from the envelope. Enclosed were two sets of documents, one handwritten in Latin, and the other typed in English, though the second bore His Holiness' personal signature as well.

"How very kind of him, he had it translated to English for

me." My face wore a sheepish grin. "You do read Latin, do you not, Deacon Brown?"

"I would be remiss if I didn't, Doctor. It is required for my vocation."

"Then you may read the Latin while I read the English." I passed the handwritten pages to him.

"Oh my," Brown said, his eyes blinking rapidly as he studied them in the sunlight of the window. "This is the Holy Father's own handwriting."

"It is indeed."

The young man swallowed hard, crossed himself, then started to read. Following his lead, I proceeded to study the English version of the pope's letter.

LEO PP. XIII

To Our dear friend

Dr. John H. Watson

Beloved Doctor, Health and Apostolic Blessing.

Regarding your inquiry about my first meeting with your dear friend Mr. Sherlock Holmes on the matter of the missing cameos, I am happy to assist you. For, after he departed my presence on that occasion, I had taken upon myself to write about the incident in my personal memoirs. During the time in question, my friend and yours spoke of how your help would have been invaluable to him, saying further how he greatly missed your company. And so, even as I accompanied him throughout the case, I volunteered, if you will pardon my presumption, to be his "Watson" for the duration. For, as the Angelic Doctor Thomas Aquinas wrote: "Friendship is the source of the greatest pleasures, and without friends even the most agreeable pursuits become tedious."

Mr. Holmes, being the gentleman he is, took my offer of inadequate assistance in great charity, for I know I am but a poor substitute for a friend such as yourself to him. Though I am certain he did not foresee that when I took this role, I understood that a requirement of it included acting as chronicler for his marvellous art, just as you would do.

And so, when all was done, I took up my pen. But as I wrote the account, it became clear that the climate of our age would be ill receptive to the tale, and some information might be compromising to your

57

friend. I decided, therefore, to hold it until which time England might be more accepting of what it revealed.

And yet, with your asking, and having met you and found you to be an amiable gentleman and one well-trusted by your friend, I send it to you. I have had it translated to English so you might not trouble yourself with it. However, I must entreat you not to publish it at this time, particularly for your friend's sake. Should England in the future prove to be more open to its content, it may be released with my heartfelt blessing.

As always, it is a joy to assist you, and I look forward to hearing from you again.

We very lovingly in the Lord impart to you again Our apostolic blessing and request the intercession of the Archangel Raphael for all your intentions.

Given at Rome in the Apostolic Palace, on the 14th day of August in the year 1895, the eighteenth of Our pontificate.

: Leo P. P. XIII :

"Imagine that! The dear old man has written his own account," I said. "He asks not to publish it, but I wonder what I should do if it were ever to be published. I shan't rewrite it."

"I would hope not," Brown said. "One does not redact a pope."

"Indeed. I wonder what my publisher would do—if he'd publish it as is and send the proper compensation to the Holy See?"

"It would be the first time the Holy Father would be published in narrative," the seminarian pointed out.

"Here, Deacon Brown," I said. "In as much as you are a faithful follower of the author, and an admirer of my friend, I would be most happy to give you the Latin version in your hands as an ordination gift."

"Sir!" He sat up straight in his chair. "You couldn't possibly. This was handwritten by His Holiness."

"The English version will suit my purposes quite well. If it ever does see print, my publisher may hunt you down to release a foreign language edition. But barring that, it is yours."

"I don't know what to say," the young man said. "Other than —thank you."

"You needn't say anything at all. Just help yourself to the scones, and let's get on with our reading. I'm just as curious as you are to read what His Holiness, Leo XIII, has to say about Sherlock Holmes and the missing Vatican Cameos."

SEQUENTIA

Editor's Note (2010): In his personal memoirs, His Holiness sometimes switches between the singular "I" to the royal "We" when referring to himself in his role as Pontiff as opposed to himself as an individual. When this occurs, the royal "We" has been rendered upper case for the sake of clarity. Other than this change, His Holiness's account of the Vatican Cameos is published here without alteration from the original English translation.

LEO PP. XIII — *personal memoir, 30th day of June in the year 1888, the eleventh of Our pontificate.*

It was late in the fifth month of 1888 that I was blessed to make the acquaintance of a fascinating young Englishman named Sherlock Holmes, who came to me by way of a problem that was sadly of my own making—albeit one made with the best of intentions.

Throughout my life, I have often in prayer placed into the hands of the Saviour the people of Britain, whose Queen Victoria, like me, had celebrated her jubilee in the year previous. How coincidental it is that she and I found our vocations concurrently, for she took her throne in June of 1837 and I was ordained on the thirty-first day of December in that same year.

Six years after becoming a priest, I, then a newly consecrated bishop, was dispatched to Victoria's uncle Leopold I, King of Belgium, as the Papal Nuncio to Brussels with the title of Archbishop of Damietta. Leopold came to hold a brotherly, if not fatherly, affection for me, and his dear wife Queen Louise, a loving, devout Catholic woman, greatly valued my spiritual guidance for her family. In 1846, I was assigned to the See of Perugia after three years in Leopold's court. And so I was off from Belgium to Rome before proceeding to Perugia, a hotbed of the revolutionary Italian anti-Catholic movement.

After leaving Brussels, however, I travelled first to England for the month of February at Leopold's recommendation to meet his esteemed royal niece, accepting the hospitality of Monsignor Wiseman, the President of Oscott Seminary.

I must admit I do not believe Her Majesty would recall that early February meeting, for I was more inclined to remember it than she would have been. She was a young woman of twenty-seven—but the spirited, wilful ruler of an empire. And I was, though noble by birth, a gangly Roman bishop who spoke to her in French so accented she had difficulty understanding me.

Forty-two years later, she still rules her empire, one much grander than when she began. And I—well, I must say I never could have predicted I would be where I am now. (Though my older brother Giuseppe states with certainty that he believed I would be here from childhood.)

Regardless, the meeting with Victoria burned an image in my mind—a comely young mother who smiled politely and was very gracious, but who held in her light eyes the shadow of dark suspicion. She saw my collar, heard my accent, knew what I was and reviled it. Not my own person necessarily, but what I represented. I went from her presence into the late winter of London, wondering what was to come of the Catholic faith in Britain—so concerned was I of her reaction to me.

For a Roman, experiencing the damp chill of England for the rest of that February was dreadful to say the least. I caught a cold which threatened to curtail my visit, but it passed with enough time for Wiseman to introduce me to two anxious new converts from the Oxford Movement, John Henry Newman and Ambrose St. John, both of whom were following vocations of their own to Oscott. The three of us spent two days getting along famously through conversing in French and Latin, walking through the frosty streets of London before travelling to the seminary together. They took me through the slums of London where the Irish population struggled to maintain faith and livelihood in a hostile culture. We then went to Tyburn where we brazenly prayed the rosary shivering in wet cold of early morning on the location where the gallows stood—though Newman was considerably more nervous about it than his brash friend who had suggested it. Upon reaching the fourth sorrowful mystery, I glanced up to see Newman's grey eyes misting with tears, gazing into my own.

"What we need, Your Excellency," he said to me, interrupting our prayer. "Is a cathedral. Right here."

St. John chuckled. "Got to have some bishops in place, first, Newman. Don't put the cart before the horse."

"If God wills it," I said, for it was the only thing I could say of which I was certain, "It will be."

I was therefore overjoyed when, after thirty-eight years, Archbishop of Westminster, Cardinal Manning wrote Us to declare he had purchased land in Westminster not far from Tyburn to build a new Catholic cathedral. It had once been the location of a prison—how fitting, since Our Lord came to preach freedom to prisoners. Our Cardinal Newman was delighted as well. And yet—there remained the dubious eyes of Victoria gazing at me in my memory. Would she allow it, or fight its completion fearing ultramontane influence on her people?

It was partly with this concern in mind that for Victoria's jubilee three years later We sent Monsignor Ruffo-Scilla to her court as an envoy with Our congratulations, prayers, and kind wishes. He was well received, or so I believed, for she dispatched in return the Catholic Duke of Norfolk Henry Fitzalan-Howard with equally kind of congratulations for my own sacerdotal jubilee.

However, in April of this, the following, year, Manning wrote to report that while he was successfully gathering funds to lay the cathedral's cornerstone, he was being met with some political opposition that threatened to halt the building's progress. It was then We decided to expand our amicable discourse with the queen in the hopes that if she was still leery of Us, at the very least she would allow the cathedral to proceed without further impediment. We wanted to make a gesture to her people, something that told her the truth of the matter— that We meant no ill will to her or her kingdom. In fact, We loved and cherished it, and only wished to serve the flock that resided there. But how does one communicate this over a distance of many miles and three hundred and fifty-four years of spiritual separation?

Having no ideas of my own for an appropriate offering of friendship, I consulted the curator of the Vatican Museum, Signore Michele Tildano. Surely we had something there that Victoria would treasure for her people (short of sending her Henry VIII's petition for a decree of nullity). Tildano was elated, for he had an idea almost immediately upon my asking.

"Holiness, I know just the thing. Cameos!"

"Cameos?"

"Queen Victoria is greatly enamoured of cameos. She wears one every day, so I've been told. Most in her collection are Italian made."

"And we have cameos?"

"Holiness, not only do we have cameos." His dark eyes glistened. "We have a small collection of Roman cameos that date from the third century B.C. to first century A.D.! It is an assortment given to Pio Nono for the Lateran Profane Museum by one of the noble families here in Rome. We've not yet displayed them in the gallery. While no curator wants to part with valuable pieces such as these, they could very well serve your needs."

"We would see these cameos, Signore."

"Without question, Holiness. I'll retrieve them now."

He brought the artworks to me in my study in a black, flat, hard-side case—seven of them all told. Fragile and priceless, resting on black velvet, they bore the images of Roman gods and emperors. The fingers of my right hand brushed over the piece with Nero's likeness carved in conch shell—he who had executed Our most blessed predecessor Saint Peter.

"Extraordinary," I said. "And easily transported to Britain by courier."

"That's my thought exactly, Holiness. Victoria would have them for her British Museum in only a few days by train."

"Excellent. We will draft a letter to Her Majesty and send a telegram to Cardinal Manning to expect the courier, as he would want to escort him personally to the presence of the queen. Can you have a courier engaged as soon as possible?"

"Absolutely, Holiness. We can have one leave at the start of the week."

And so it was that the cameos were on their way to England on Tuesday, the twenty-second of May, heralded by a letter to Victoria herself in Our hand and stamped with Our seal. In it, We expressed Our love to the British people and the hope that the cameos would be accepted as a gift to enrich the lives of all of Queen Victoria's subjects.

As I waited to hear word of the cameos' reception, I plunged into my work—Our latest encyclical on human liberty. Three days later, as I worked with my Latinist prelate Monsignor Tarozzi in editing that document, my personal chamberlain Pio Centra escorted a young seminarian into my study. He was clearly terrified to be in my presence, and was clutching in his hand a yellow sheet of paper—a telegram.

"Brother Giocomo Dionisio, Holiness," Pio said. "A Jesuit seminarian. He assists at the telegraph office."

I looked over my spectacles at the youth. "*Buon giorno,* Brother Giocomo. That is for me, no?"

He knelt at my knee and reverenced Our fisherman's ring. "Holy Father, please assure me you'll remain calm."

Of course, when someone says this, it is the last thing one does. "Calm? What has happened?"

"I recorded this message myself and ran all the way here once I read it. Holiness—did you send some valuables to Queen Victoria?"

"Yes. They arrived?"

He shook his head. "They're missing."

I felt the blood drain from my face. "What?"

"When they opened the case it was empty."

"No." I could scarcely breathe nor blink. "Tell me she was not present for this."

The young man held out the paper to me in a trembling hand, and I took it from him.

63

BUCKINGHAM PALACE
25. MAY 1888
TO: LEO PP.XIII
Courier arrived with case, but no items were within. Courier being questioned at present. He denies wrongdoing. H.M. desires full investigation. Please advise.
—H.E. CARDINAL MANNING
Via H.Ponsonby, Secretary to H.R.M., V.R.

From Victoria's personal secretary—she had indeed opened the case with Manning in attendance. It stood to reason she would of course, for I would have.

"Summon Tildano," I said, my voice barely audible to me for my heart pounding.

The young man at my knee looked confused. "Who, Holy Father?"

"Signore Tildano. The curator of the museum. Fetch him for me, quickly."

Brother Giocomo nodded and dashed out the door, and for a moment I was envious of youth, that it could move with such speed. For my own part, I slumped in my chair, removed my reading spectacles and rubbed my eyes. I knew royalty—for I was raised in that realm, educated in their schools, and had moved among them throughout my career. All were capricious to some degree and Victoria, despite her own rumoured steadfastness and justice, could possibly be as petty as any other. Mistakes of this sort were unacceptable in these circles, intentional or not. Any hope I had of touching her heart now seemed irrevocably lost.

"Holiness," said Tarozzi from the desk. "Are you all right?"

"No."

"Shall I fetch your physician?"

"No."

At that moment the bells of the Angelus tolled at St. Peter's. I slid from my chair to kneel and pray. Tarozzi followed suit, coming around the desk to kneel beside me. We made the sign of the cross and began. But as we spoke together the words of the ancient devotion, my concern about the cameos weighed heavily upon me, influencing my silent prayer.

"Angelus Domini nuntiavit Mariae…."

Sweet Mother of Christ hear me, I silently prayed, and place my worries at the feet of your son,

"…Ave Maria, gratia plena; Dominus tecum: benedicta tu in mulieribus, et benedictus fructus ventris tui Iesus…."

I only desire to shepherd His children well, plead to Him who is God incarnate on my behalf.

"…Ecce ancilla Domini…"

I place all my care and worry in your Immaculate Heart for you understand such suffering.

"…Et Verbum caro factum est…"

Lord, to whom shall I go?

"…Ora pro nobis, sancta Dei Genetrix…"

In you O Lord, I have my strength.

"….Per eumdem Christum Dominum nostrum. Amen."

My face was in my hands. Tarozzi made the sign of the cross next to me, and noticed my posture. "Holiness," he said. "Let me help you."

I wiped my hands down my face. "Allow me a few moments alone, Monsignor, if you please."

He rose and held out his hand. "At least let me help you stand."

I waved him away. "I want to stay here. Give me some time to collect myself. If Brother Giocomo returns with the curator, tell Pio he may send them in."

"Yes, Your Holiness."

After he left, I rested my face in my hands again, leaning my elbows on my chair to pray. Twenty minutes later, I heard a knock at the door. "Come."

Brother Giocomo and Tildano entered together, but stopped when they saw me on my knees. "Should we come back, Holy Father?" Giocomo asked.

"No, come here and help me stand, young man." He did as I ordered, supporting me with a strong arm. "Now, Signore," I said to Tildano, straightening my cassock. "Perhaps you can give me an explanation as to why the cameos were not in the case when they reached Victoria?"

Tildano, pale as a sheet of new paper, shook his head. "I have none, Your Holiness."

"None?" An edge of frustration caused my voice to become sharp. "You must do better than that, Signore."

"Holiness, I checked the case personally. I saw they were well affixed inside so they would not tumble about. I placed your note in the case, closed it and locked it. I then gave it to the courier. I cannot for the life of me explain why they were not in there."

"And yet this same courier arrives in London with an empty case and shamelessly opens it in the presence of the Queen. This does not sound like the actions of a guilty man."

"He has a most excellent reputation for trustworthiness, Holy Father."

"Then where on Earth *are* they?!"

Tildano only opened his mouth and closed it, clearly as flummoxed as I was. I started to pace back and forth, tapping my forehead with my knuckle. Something was terribly wrong with this whole scenario, but I was not seeing it. I stopped pacing next to the desk and sat down, taking up the pen. Dipping it in the inkwell, I wrote in French on a spare piece of foolscap:

> To: H.R.M., V.R.
>
> We are deeply dismayed by these circumstances. Our curator insists the items left here well secure and in trustworthy care. We, too, desire an investigation, though We would be immensely grateful for any assistance as Our capabilities in that area are limited.
>
> In all humility, We implore Your patience and forgiveness as We work together for a positive resolution to this matter.
>
> In the love of the most merciful Saviour,
>
> LEO PP. XIII

I handed the paper to Brother Giocomo. "Send this in its entirety with a copy to Cardinal Manning. I know it is verbose for a telegram, but each word is important. Come to me as soon as you have a response. It does not matter when it is—unless I'm celebrating Mass, of course. I'll be waiting for it."

"Certainly, Holy Father."

As Giocomo left, I looked up at Tildano. "Go back to your museum, Signore, and set your people to a search. If they are still there, I'll have to find some very fine words in way of an

66

apology." I sighed and rested my head in my hand. "I work well with words, but am I that gifted?"

Tildano did not respond to my rhetorical question. "I'll report to you if I find anything, Holy Father."

I waved him away, and as the door closed, I gazed down at the pages of my encyclical before me—its words blurring before my eyes. I realised I had removed my reading glasses. Glancing around for them, I saw that I had laid them on my chair when I'd knelt to pray. But now I had no energy to stand and retrieve them. Weariness rested like a lead weight upon my shoulders. My gaze then fixed on the small Byzantine image of Our Lady of Perpetual Succour that rested on my desk—the Blessed Mother giving comfort to a frightened child Jesus as Gabriel and Michael hold forth the cross and spear—instruments of his divine passion. Reaching out with my fingers, I caressed the veil of the Madonna, hoping she would pass to me some of the same consolation.

I then heard the door quietly open again. Looking up, I saw Matteo, one of the papal gentlemen and who helped care for the apartment and serve meals. He was a princely young man of noble heritage, but he had a devout innocence about him. He stood still in his black suit like a shadow, waiting to be addressed.

"What is it, Matteo?"

"Holiness," he said, his voice soft and uncertain. "Would you not like something to eat?"

I shook my head. "I am not hungry."

"But Holy Father, you had nothing but coffee for breakfast." His expression was desperate. "Surely you need something more substantial."

I released a deep sigh. My eating habits were a torture to the servants. The older ones were used to Pio Nono's appetite—he'd eaten very well, and it showed in his portly figure. I, meanwhile, fasted more often than not—a shocking aberration in a culture in which one often shows love to another by what they create for them—food in particular.

He came and knelt beside me. "Please, Holy Father, even if you eat a panini, it is better than nothing."

I rested my hand on his shoulder. "With these troubles today I have lost any appetite I had."

"If I might make a recommendation, Holy Father—?"

"I should eat anyway?"

Matteo smiled, some of his uncertainty dissolving. "Well, yes, but beyond that."

"Tell me."

"Perhaps you should ask the intercession of Blessed Rita of Cascia on the problem. I have a particular devotion to her, as she is from my home town. But she does seem to assist in the most impossible situations."

His suggestion was so ingenuous I could not help but smile. But it was not without merit. "I may just do that. Now, what have the cooks prepared for luncheon?"

"Chickpea soup with rosemary, fresh bread and if you wish, some fresh trout braised with garlic and lemon."

Despite what I'd said about a lack of appetite, the interest of my palate took over. "I would enjoy a bowl of soup and some bread."

"Right away, Holy Father." He clasped my hand and kissed my ring with grateful enthusiasm before dashing from the room.

With a deep sigh, I stood and retrieved my reading glasses before following him to the dining room. God forbid I returned and sat on them without thinking.

The soup was indeed delicious, and I noticed the sly cooks had slipped some tiny chunks of the fish into it to give me some extra nourishment. As I was finishing, the young telegraph operator rushed into the dining room, breathless from running.

"Holiness," he said, beaming. "It's wonderful news!" He knelt beside my chair and handed me the telegram in his hand.

"They've found them?"

His face fell. "Ah, no. Not that good. But good nonetheless. They're sending Sherlock Holmes!"

"Who?" The name rang so foreign in my ears. And yet—it was strangely familiar.

"A consulting detective from England, Holy Father. He has

a very keen mind, and solves the most difficult problems. He's unravelled some rather touchy situations for several of the crowned heads of Europe."

"Ah—" That explained why the name was somewhat familiar to me, though I knew little of the details. There was something I recalled of a scandalous problem with the royal family of Holland. I took up my reading glasses that I'd set by my water glass and slipped them on to read the telegram.

Buckingham Palace
25. May 1888
To: Leo PP. XIII
    We are sending Mr. Sherlock Holmes to you, a consulting detective of impeccable reputation who has Our complete trust. You may expect him on Monday a.m., 28 May. We are certain that if he cannot find the missing items for us, no one can. In the meantime, be assured of Our fond wishes.
                                —V.R.

Relief at her gentle response caused me to melt into my chair. "She composed this herself," I said.

"You did the same, Holiness. I suppose she wanted to return the gesture."

"How very gracious. Perhaps I've misjudged her." I noticed the young man's eyes studying my soup dish. "Have you eaten yet, Brother?"

"Not yet, Holy Father. I was waiting at the telegraph."

"Sit." I said, pointing to the chair cornerwise to my own.

He looked uncomfortable at my command. It was not customary for subordinates to sit in my presence, and yet, he could do nothing but obey.

"Matteo," I called.

Matteo entered from the serving room.

"Please bring this young man some of your soup and fish. He has worked hard for me today running back and forth."

After Giocomo was served and said his prayer of thanks, I asked, "So tell me, how do you know of this Sherlock Holmes?" I repeated the name; pronouncing it was difficult to my lips. "Sherlock Holmes. What an impossible name to say. Why is it these English wrap all their words in such doggerel consonants?"

Brother Giocomo laughed, then sobered quickly. "Excuse me, Holy Father."

"For what? I was trying to be amusing. It must be the curse of the papacy that no one laughs at one's jests anymore. Now, please, explain to me how you know this man."

"Well, besides the rumours one always hears flying about in a telegraph office, I read about him in a magazine."

"A magazine?"

"Yes, his friend, a Dr. John H. Watson, composed a serial narrative of one of his cases. It was published in translation in two instalments here in Italy. It is called *A Study in Scarlet*."

"It sounds like a boudoir novel!"

The young man looked abashed. "Hardly that, Holy Father. It's a mystery that tells of how Signore Holmes uses the science of deduction to solve a murder case."

"Is that so? I would read this story. Do you still have it?"

"Yes, Holiness."

"After you finish your lunch, We will send a 'thank you' reply to Her Majesty. Then please bring this story to me. I will read it as I lie down for siesta."

COMMUNIO

Over the next three days I found time throughout my busy schedule to read the tale Giocomo brought me and found myself looking forward to meeting this young Englishman of such remarkable intellectual talents. I also made a point during my private devotions to ask the intercession of Blessed Rita of Cascia on the problem as Matteo suggested.

True to Victoria's promise, the much heralded Sherlock Holmes arrived on Monday morning around ten thirty. It was, by coincidence, the feast of Augustine of Canterbury, the saint and confessor who converted the people of Britain to Christianity. I wondered if this might be a sign of Divine Providence.

I had cleared my schedule for most of the day in anticipation

70

HE STOOD BEFORE ME WEARING AN ALOOF EXPRESSION.

of Signore Holmes' visit, but still I tried to finish as much work as I could before his arrival. My High Chamberlain Monsignor Macchi escorted him into my study as I was finishing up some last minute items with Tarozzi. The detective was, as his biographer described, an imposing, slender gentleman in his early thirties, with sharp features and slightly receding hairline. Dressed in a pristine grey, tweed suit, he held a short-brimmed homburg hat, and a finely-moulded gold ring suggestive of royal patronage sparkled on the fourth finger of his right hand. In his opposite hand he held an ebony, silver-tipped walking stick. From my vantage point in my chair it seemed he nearly scraped the top of the door frame with his head—though likely he missed it by a few inches. He stood before me wearing an aloof expression, and his cool, grey eyes darted about, taking everything in—absorbing the setting with a piercing gaze.

I must briefly note that while Signore Holmes spoke to me in what I'd best describe as satisfactory book-learned Italian, he would sometimes slip into Latin when he failed to remember a word or verb conjugation. For some around me this switch was jarring, and they'd fail to understand him. But being fluent in both languages, I understood him quite well. I will therefore render his speech in its meaning, rather than how it was literally spoken to me.

After Macchi announced Holmes, I tilted my head forward to study him over my reading glasses. "*Buon giorno*, Signore Holmes, *piacere*. You are quite tall." I held out my hand, for even Protestants recognise Us with a gentle reverence.

Out of the corner of my eyes, I noticed the monsignor at my shoulder, slightly bending his knees, indicating to the Englishman that he should kneel.

The young man seemed not to notice. He took two steps into the room and said in a trenchant, tenor voice, "Your Holiness, I am pleased to make your acquaintance as well. Before we proceed on ceremony, I must ask you if you'd prefer those who deal with you to be honest or dishonest."

I raised my eyebrows and dropped my hand to the armrest of my chair. "Honest, of course."

"Then I must tell you that I am a loyal subject of Her Majesty Queen Victoria, Supreme Governor of the Church of England. While I do not wish to insult Your Holiness by forgoing the time immemorial tradition of kneeling to kiss your hand, I think it would be disingenuous for me to make such a gesture. It would begin our friendship with a base of dishonesty."

"Ah." I glanced over at Tarozzi and Macchi, the faces of whom had turned ashen with what they no doubt perceived to be an insult to Our person.

In truth, I was not insulted, merely saddened. For while the Englishman spoke of an allegiance to his Queen over Us, I perceived that it was more personal pride. Positions of prestige meant little to one such as he who gloried in the intellect he'd conditioned to his own set of standards, even the exalted station of the Vicar of Christ on Earth. I realised that to him, respect was something earned, and for my part I understood.

I removed my spectacles and handed them and the volume in my lap to Macchi, then moved to stand up. However, I'd sat in one position for too long—my joints were uncomfortably frozen. "Come here, my son," I said, beckoning to the Englishman.

He did as I asked and moved to the left of my chair.

"Please help me to stand."

He took my arm, giving me the added support I needed to rise. "*Grazie*, Signore." I am considered tall among Italians at nearly five feet ten inches, but he seemed to tower above me. "*Allora*," I said, smiling up at him. "My first impression of you is as I said. I must strain my neck to look up at you. Pray tell me, what is your height?"

"A bit over six feet, Your Holiness."

"Gracious! What did your mother feed you?"

A slight smile finally crossed his face that had been without humour as he entered. "My mother had me eat everything whether I wanted to or not."

I grunted with amusement. "Yours and mine both. Is it not miraculous that as men we are thin as reeds?"

Turning to Tarozzi, I gave him a dismissive wave. "Monsignor, we will continue this later. Go have some breakfast with Monsignor Macchi and let the signore have your chair."

The bishop looked back and forth between the two of us. He then took up his things, offering the Englishman his place as he left in a flutter of robes along with his brother bishop. Holmes walked behind the desk and placed his hat and stick upon it. He did not sit down, but instead studied the books upon my shelves with his hands clasped behind his back.

After Tarozzi walked out the door with Macchi, I noticed another very nervous moustached young man standing just outside the door. He was gripping a brown bowler in his hands so tightly as if to rend it in two.

"And who are you, my son?" I asked.

"My apologies, Holiness," Sherlock Holmes said, turning back to me. "This is Signore Vicini, the courier—"

Vicini rushed forward to kneel before me. He kissed my ring, and then dropped his head to kiss the top of my slipper with an expression of profound shame. "I am the one who lost the cameos, Holy Father. Pray, forgive me."

"Vicini," Holmes said, an impatient edge to his voice. "I

have already told you that you did not lose them. Now please, contain yourself."

I rested my right hand gently on Vicini's bowed head to bless him and looked over at the Englishman. "If he did not lose them, Signore, then where did they go?"

"Nowhere. They are here."

"Here?"

"When you have eliminated the impossible, whatever remains, however improbable, must be the truth. They were not with Vicini when he arrived in London, though the case he brought had not been out of his possession at any time. Therefore he did not leave with them in the first place." He tapped his long fingers on the desk. "They're here, or at least were. Where they are now, I'm not certain. That, of course, is what I need to determine."

"There, you see," I said, looking down at the man at my feet. "If Signore Holmes says you did not lose them, then you did not. Now," I continued gently, "I would like to speak to the signore for a few moments. Would you please wait outside?"

"Yes, Holy Father." He picked himself up from the floor and scampered out the door, closing it behind him.

"He is very guilt-ridden," I observed.

"And it has been an exceptional pleasure travelling with him for three days, I assure you."

I did my best to suppress a smile at his sarcasm, but I wasn't entirely successful. "Please sit, Signore. I wish to stand for a bit to move my legs."

He did as I requested, though I noticed his scrutinizing gaze once again making its way around the room, over my desk, and back to me as I paced to the window loggia facing out onto the Piazza of Saint Peter. It was a beautiful morning. The warm yellow sun was casting decorative shadows of the saints' statues upon the stone pavement below.

Turning back at him, I said, "You study me, Signore. Is it true that you can see all there is about a man when you look at him?"

"One may observe and conclude much, Holiness. I would hesitate to say all."

"What do you see about me, then?"

74

He sighed with what I perceived to be either annoyance or impatience, then answered me in a quick staccato, "Other than the facts that Your Holiness eats very little, takes snuff, has a great dependence upon the works of Thomas Aquinas, an exceptional knowledge of Latin, entertains a marked interest in scientific research, is devoted to the Madonna, enjoys chess, writes incessantly, and presently suffers from insomnia, I can discern nothing else that would not be plainly obvious to most observers."

"I am the Pope, you mean."

"Yes." A mild smile once again crossed his face.

"*Va Bene,*" I said. "Let me see if I can determine how you learned these things." I folded my arms. "I am considered far too thin, an indication I eat little. The snuff box on the desk is a sign of my occasional use of snuff. The well-worn condition of my Aquinas texts shows that I use them frequently, and the documents in Latin on the desk demonstrate my expertise in Latin. The images of Our Lady and the rosary on my desk suggest my devotion to her. My collection of science texts signifies an interest in that field of study, and my chess set in the corner with a configuration of a finished game which I *won*," I winked slyly, "reveals my love of chess."

The gentleman's marginal smile widened a bit. "You have me at my own game, Your Holiness."

"Not entirely. You said I write incessantly. Do you know this because of my encyclicals?"

Holmes shook his head. "The stain of ink and indentation on the tip of your right index finger indicates one whose pen rarely leaves his hand."

I glanced at my ink-stained finger. "Marvellous. And insomnia?"

"The insomnia one can read in your face. You do not look well-rested. But if one were not looking at you, we'd observe it from the candles and quills."

"Candles and quills?"

He pushed forward the candle stand that sat on the desk. "This candle was replaced in the morning hours just before dawn for it is barely burned. There is also an accumulation of wax around its base, showing that the stand was not scraped before a new candle was placed—something a servant would do. Therefore a servant did not replace the candle, you did because they were asleep at the time. You were awake most of the night working. Indeed, as I see now—most of these written pages here are in a different hand than that of His Excellency who used the pen he took with him. The remaining quill is well covered in ink that is still somewhat fresh; therefore I would think it had been used most the night."

"Excellent," I said. "I have often been working through the night. You have a blessed gift, Signore."

"Thank you, Holiness." The Englishman then pursed his lips. "Is there something else?"

"Yes." He leaned forward with his elbows on my desk. "I need to make a request of you. It has no relevance to the case, but if I do not ask you now I will not remember once my mind is fully engaged on the problem at hand."

"Please do. Of course, little we've discussed so far has any bearing on this case."

He waved his hand. "All that is necessary with a new client," he said. "This is different."

"Then pray, tell me what it is."

He sighed and seemed uncertain of what he was about to say. "My dear friend Dr. Watson—"

"Ah yes, your biographer."

"You know of him?"

"When I was told you were coming, I read *A Study in Scarlet* at the recommendation of one of my people."

Holmes groaned and wiped his hand over his head.

"Is the account not true, Signore?"

"Oh, it's true. But he writes in such a sensational way. I would have preferred a scientific paper on the situation."

"Well." I chuckled. "I'll agree that it was a little melodramatic. But a scientific paper would certainly not win public admiration. And he writes out of love of you. Surely you can appreciate that much."

He blinked thoughtfully at my sentiment. "I suppose."

"Nonetheless, we are veering from the point. What is it the dear doctor wishes of me?"

"He feared for the life of a patient and her child. She is a wife of a good friend of his and she and her family are part of your flock. He asked that you pray for her."

"She is in childbed?"

"Yes."

"What is her name?"

"Mrs. Genevieve Murray."

"She is of Irish descent?"

"Yes."

"I would be most happy to pray for her during my devotions, and I will offer Mass for her tomorrow. Would that be sufficient?"

"More than sufficient, Holiness."

"If I may ask, have you and your friend not prayed for her yourselves?"

He shook his head. "We are not men of faith, Your Holiness."

I nodded sadly, suspecting as much. In this day, agnosticism or atheism often accompanied those in scientific study. We hoped to encourage the opposite throughout Our pontificate. "Perhaps you should take up my well-used quill there and write a telegram to your friend? I assume Dr. Watson asked because the lady believes in the power of prayer and he hopes her belief will ferry her through the danger. A written confirmation of my involvement would best serve his medical purposes, no?"

Holmes pondered this only a short moment, then took up my pen.

I tugged the bell pull next to the window, and Pio entered. "Signore Holmes has a telegram to send, Pio. Please have one of the gentlemen take it over to Brother Giocomo. He's proven he's efficient and trustworthy at the telegraph."

Pio took the paper the Englishman offered him.

"And Pio," I added. "When you finish with that, bring me my cappello and walking stick."

"You are going out, Holy Father?"

"I wish to escort the signore over to the museum. It seems to be a lovely day, and I thought maybe we could go by way of the gardens." I motioned for him to go then returned my gaze to

Holmes. "You don't mind if we walk a few extra steps, do you Signore?"

He gave a dismissive shrug. "A small delay makes little difference now. The scene has already been disturbed. I'll have to recreate events."

"I fail to follow you."

"It's been a nearly a week since the incident that caused the cameos to be missing occurred. In that time, regular business went on and then searches were conducted all around the area in which the cameos were packaged. This disrupts any evidence I might find. It makes the whole process of investigation more difficult, but not impossible. In any case, a little extra time spent taking a route through the gardens is going to make no difference at this point."

"Hm." I frowned. "If I'd realised this, I'd not have insisted a search be conducted, and I'd have placed the area under guard."

"You acted properly, Holiness. What if they'd been found? It would not be necessary for me to be here at all."

Pio returned with my white, brimmed cappello and carved redwood walking stick. Placing the hat on my head over my zucchetto, I looked around the room. "Now where did I put my reading glasses?"

Pio held them out to me.

"Ah, grazie." I placed them in my right pocket. "Shall we go then, Signore?"

He followed me from my study into the sitting room, putting on his own hat as he did so. The courier waiting outside leaped from the settee near the window facing us. "Signore Vicini," I said to him. "Go ahead of us and tell Signore Tildano we're on our way there. I'd rather they not be surprised when we walk in—"

"Wait, Holiness," said Holmes.

"What?"

"It's best they be surprised. If this is a case of employee thievery, the thief is best caught off guard. It may cause him to make a mistake that I'll notice."

"Excellent point." I turned again to the nervous courier. "Are you married, Signore Vicini?"

"Yes, Holiness. I have two children as well."

"I assume you have the information you need from him?" I asked Holmes.

"Three days worth."

"Then go home to your family, my son. Assure them of my best wishes. If I have any need of you, I'll summon you right away."

"*Grazie*, Holiness." The courier bowed and left quickly.

Escorted by four of the Pontifical Guard in their Prussian-style helmets—two halberdiers and two officers carrying swords and pistols—I walked together with the Englishman down two flights of stairs, through the Apostolic Palace, past the Courtyard of San Damaso and on to the Sistine Chapel via several private passageways. As I led him, his longer, more youthful strides caused me to move a little faster than I was accustomed, but I did not mind. It did me good, I thought, to move my legs. The chapel has an exit from the rear that leads to the Piazza del Forno and the Papal Gardens, so I led him casually into the chapel, failing to realise that he'd probably never seen it before. He slowed to a stop, gazing all around him, then up at the ceiling. His eyes were wide with awe.

"I had absolutely no idea," he said.

I smiled. "That's what I said when I first saw it."

"One could spend hours just studying all of this."

"Some have." I gazed up at the ceiling with him.

"When I was fifteen, my family passed through Rome as part of our extended European tour. I greatly desired to see this room then, but it did not fit into the family schedule. Throughout my adult life I've refused to fill my mind with superfluous subjects for what was necessary in my field of study, but I still wanted to see this." His eyes locked on the Last Judgement, and he stepped closer to gaze at its sprawling majesty. "The skin, there—" With his walking stick he pointed at a bearded figure in the centre of the painting holding the skin of a man that had been flayed. "That's believed to be Michelangelo himself?"

"Yes. I'm afraid Our predecessor Julius II was a bit hard on him. No doubt Buonorotti felt he was in Hell as he worked. Though, as the Angelic Doctor wrote, 'The test of the artist does not lie in the will with which he goes to work, but in the excellence of the work he produces.'"

"Angelic Doctor?" He gave me a quizzical look.

"Aquinas," I said.

He grunted.

"A philosopher. Your friend indicated in his narrative that you knew nothing of philosophy."

"My friend underestimated the limits of my knowledge to some extent. I read Aquinas years ago in school."

"But you let it slip from your mind as you did Dr. Watson's description of the solar system."

"It does not influence what I do." He said simply, raising an eyebrow.

"It does not influence—?" I dropped the tip of my walking stick on the marble floor, and the thump reverberated around the colourful, frescoed walls of the chapel. "Young man, Thomas Aquinas is one of the great fathers of logical reasoning along with Aristotle and Plato. His method of thought helped form the basis of modern science. It is shocking that you do not realise that."

Holmes' eyebrows furrowed. He seemed disturbed by my words. Philosophy didn't fit within his view of the world around him, and yet—it was integral to it.

"I assume," I said. "That you are more agnostic than atheist, is that so?"

"I would never deny that God exists. I would merely assert that he cannot be proven."

"I would disagree, of course. He can be proven from nature through human reason."

He did not look convinced.

"Tell me," I pointed to the large figure in the middle of the painting. "What is your opinion of him?"

"Christ? I have none."

"None at all? I would think he'd present a fascinating problem for you to unravel."

"How so?"

I shrugged. "Well, one who makes the claim of being the Son of God could only be a madman or liar, no? And being either, he could not be a 'great moral teacher' as some have claimed. You said yourself, Signore, 'When you have eliminated the impossible, whatever remains,—' What was the rest of it?"

"—however improbable, must be the truth."

"Yes, yes. Would it not be impossible for one who is insane or a liar to be such a great moral teacher as to form society's values as he has? It strikes at the core of who we are, even of you, who do not believe. It stands to reason that if he cannot be a great moral teacher for these things, then whatever remains, however improbable, must be the truth and that he was—"

"—who he claimed to be." Holmes returned his gaze to the painting and was silent a full moment before speaking again. "Holiness, you are an exceptionally clever man. Your argument is masterfully executed, but it is based on a false premise."

"Which is?" I smiled.

"Insanity or truthfulness does not mean one cannot have great influence on society."

"My son, you are equating 'moral teacher' with 'influential person.' The two are not the same, nor are morals the result of influence. Morals are truths that attract recognition when presented clearly. A liar, well, how would we know what was truth from him moral or otherwise? And an insane man, while he may be influential, could not properly, or at least consistently, form cogent moral truths to attract the proper recognition. Like a broken clock either of them may be right at least twice a day, but is that a clock by which you'd set your pocket watch?"

Holmes' lips formed a half smile. "You are enjoying this, aren't you?"

"I am. I could match wits with you all day, but I fear I may lose."

"I'm not too certain of that," he replied. "As I said before, you are clever."

I shook my head. "Signore Holmes, if I was truly clever, I would have those bedevilling cameos by now. As it is, they are still lost and I haven't the faintest idea how to go about finding them. Solving such problems is *your* expertise, not mine." I tapped my finger at my temple. "I merely coaxed your marvellous mind beyond its self-imposed limitations in knowledge with the hope you'd realise that other schools of thought manipulate and mould those whom you observe. These things do matter, Signore." I swept my arm open wide to the paintings all around us. "They matter because they influence mankind and make him who he is. All I ask is that you not limit yourself.

"Of course," I continued, "by putting you through this exercise, I've placed a small responsibility upon you. For, as the beloved disciple John wrote, 'Whosoever shall confess that Jesus is the Son of God, God abideth in him, and he in God.' Perhaps you should spend some of your inactive time pondering *that* conundrum instead of indulging in whatever narcotic it is with which you choose to entertain yourself." I smiled with good humour and tilted my head to the door at the rear of the chapel. "Let's go to the museum, shall we?"

"I should never have let Watson publish that blasted story," Holmes muttered as he followed me into the rear passage.

"Please do not fault your friend or his work." I stopped while the guard captain ahead of us opened the door to the outside. "Watson's writings will be a great help to you in the end, as they'll increase your notoriety and therefore your business." Stepping out into the piazza, I heard the sound of the small fountain echoing about the buildings. It was indeed sunny and pleasant outside. Squinting in the brightness of the day, I led Holmes across the sun-bleached brick pavement.

"Until now I was not aware of how well Watson's story could be used against me," Holmes said.

"Used *against* you?" I paused next to the fountain to gaze up at him. A light spray of water tickled the back of my neck. "Signore, have I offended you?"

"No, Holiness." In typical English fashion, he was polite, but his lips were pressed tightly together.

"On the contrary, I see that I have. Pray forgive an old man, my son. I am a teacher, and when I encounter a brilliant mind perhaps I push too hard. Truly, I meant no insult. I find that I like you very much."

He sighed and his expression softened. "You challenged me, Holiness. I suppose I should be grateful for the mental stimulation."

"But I fear I cut a little too close to the quick in the end and for that I do apologise." We started walking apace again. Our route took us into a loggia passageway through the building on the other side of the piazza, which exited onto the garden path along the museum.

"You are correct, though," Holmes continued as we walked. "I should not fault Watson. He is a good friend and a great help to me. I'd hoped he would have joined me on this case."

"And I would have liked to have met him. Here," I said, eagerly, "while I would be a poor substitute for your friend, I would be happy to be your 'Watson' for this problem. I can be a silent sounding board, or someone from whom to solicit opinions." I placed my hand upon my breast. "I promise to curtail the theological and philosophical pontificating—if a pope can be forgiven for doing that on occasion?"

"No one would be more suited to pontificating, Holiness." A genuine smile formed on Holmes' face. "But I would be honoured to have your assistance."

"Excellent! I—" I stopped, feeling a sharp, clutching pain in my chest. I gasped, feeling the pain intensify as I did so. This was, sadly, a regular occurrence, and I should have known better as it only happened when I overexerted myself after being inactive for solid periods time, just as I had been that morning.

"What's wrong, Your Holiness?"

"Angina." My fingers clasped my pectoral cross.

"Here, guards!" Holmes called to the soldiers. "Help me get him to the bench there."

Strong arms on either side of me guided me to a grey stone seat in the garden facing the Fountain of the Sacrament. Silently I prayed the *Ave*, knowing that usually by the time I finished, the pain would subside. When I opened my eyes, I realised I'd been muttering it aloud.

I looked up to see the concerned faces of young men surrounding me, and the pain began to abate, releasing its grip upon my heart.

"Should I fetch your physician, Holy Father?" said the captain of the guard who crouched in front of me. He spoke to me in French, as several of the Swiss Guard did for often their

French was better than their Italian. His bright blue eyes were filled with worry.

"No. Just give me time to rest here," I replied in his chosen language.

"I was walking too fast," said Holmes seated next to us. His face was drawn with concern.

"*You* were walking too fast?" I said. "No, *I* was walking too fast. Who is leading whom? I'm seventy-eight, not a young one like you with legs that can leap the Tiber. When I encounter youthful energy I forget that I do not have that gift. I should have known better. Give me another moment, and then we'll continue. I do not wish to detain you much longer." I looked up at the soldiers. "Captain, I am fine now. You and your men may go—" I flicked my fingers to them, "—guard."

As they moved a small distance away to await my decision to depart, Holmes said, "You were speaking French."

"What?"

He rubbed his eyes. "Ah—I remember now. You were Papal Nuncio to Belgium. Had I remembered that, I would not have assaulted your ears with my Italian."

"My son, your Italian is very good." I smiled. "You should continue to speak it so you practice, and if you need to you may address me in French."

He gave me a weak smile. "You are very gracious, Your Holiness. Here now, what's this?"

"What's what?" Looking where his gaze was fixed—at my right arm and knee— I saw three small honey bees had decided to hover and perch. They seemed to be searching for nectar.

"*Apis mellifera ligusticae,*" he said. "Italian honey bees, though rather light in colour—almost white. There must be a hive nearby. But what is singular is that they've landed on you." He looked up at me. "Did you have anything sweet for breakfast, Holiness?"

I shook my head. "I had only coffee and a roll this morning."

"Did you have sugar in the coffee? Marmalade on the roll?"

"No. What's the matter?"

"It is merely odd that they'd cluster on your finger that way.

They look as if they're searching for nectar. I'd think you should have something that's attracting them."

I grunted. "How strange."

"Indeed."

One bee lifted in the air again, and perched upon my blue-green emerald fisherman's ring, and where he led, the others soon followed, crawling about my fingers near the gem.

"Perhaps it is the colour of the gem that's confused them," said Holmes.

I chuckled and made the sign of blessing gently over them with my left hand. "Go on, little messengers, I understand." The bees scattered.

"Understand what?"

"Blessed Rita of Cascia," I explained. "Ah, Rita, We will canonise you if you are true to Us."

"I fail to follow you."

"Bees are her sign, Signore. For three days I've asked her intercession on this cameos problem for she is a patroness of impossible situations, and three bees have come to tell me she heard. I believe she will assist you in this problem." Seeing his sceptical look, I patted him on the shoulder then used it as leverage to stand. "Come, my son." I started down the path again at a much slower pace than I'd taken previously.

The path followed the side of the Museum. All along the wall, the gardeners had been at work pulling out old, blight-ridden hedges that had at one time grown so voluminous as to block the first floor windows to the museum offices. Fresh soil was scattered onto the brick path and open holes from the removed bushes lined the length of the brick walkway. When we reached the bushes they'd not yet removed, Holmes stopped and pointed with his stick.

"There's the hive there. No wonder they halted their project."

Sure enough, the hive was nestled between the wall and the old bush, surrounded by the darting, buzzing creatures.

"Yes, that is a delicate situation, no?" I pointed to a single door just beyond the hedge. "Anyone who comes out that door may have a surprise."

"If your gardener is wise they'll preserve and cultivate the hive so the papal household will have fresh honey."

"I believe we have a beekeeper on premises already."

"He should handle it, then. Moving a hive without experience can be a dangerous business."

We continued on, and a few hundred feet further down the wall was another entrance into the first floor offices beneath the Hall of Sixtus V and the Apostolic Library. The guard captain at the front of our party opened the door for us and I stepped into the hallway. But I halted at the hall intersection, wondering for a moment which way to turn.

"The curator's office is this way?" I asked the officer, pointing ahead of us.

"Yes, Holiness. I'll show you."

I glanced up at my new friend with a sheepish expression. "I haven't been down here since I was a cardinal."

The officer led us down the hall into a large workroom, in which museum employees garbed in white aprons and gloves were cleaning various pieces of art at work tables. The halberdiers took up positions on either side of the door. When they snapped their halberds at attention, all the faces in the room raised to look at us. Expressions of horror, shock, and alarm were plain as all present dropped to their knees.

"Allow your friend to keep writing his stories, Signore," I said to Holmes *sotto voce*, "And they'll do this for *you*."

"God forbid," Holmes muttered.

Just then Tildano entered from an office on the side of the room. Surprised, he went to his knee before me and kissed my ring. "Holiness, we didn't know you were coming—"

"I know," I said, gesturing for him to rise. "This gentleman," I said, indicating the Englishman, "is Signore Sherlock Holmes, sent by her Majesty Queen Victoria to assist us in recovering the cameos."

"Signore Holmes, it is a pleasure," said Tildano, shaking his hand.

"You are to obey him as you'd obey me in this case, with the exception, of course, of ring veneration and kneeling." I looked to Holmes with a raised eyebrow. "Unless you desire it, Signore?"

"I think we can forgo that formality, Holiness."

"*Va bene.* I will now step aside and let you command."

Holmes nodded. "If you'd be so kind, Signore Tildano, I'd like to see where you packaged the cameos to go to England."

Tildano led us to through a door at back of the room, and into a large storage area. A grey marble counter lined the corner and wall to our left, and wood shelves layered with hard-backed storage cases and pull out wire baskets went back for several hundred feet. A card catalogue with four rows of drawers lined the opposite wall next to a dark hard wood desk. Gas lamps lit the room, though a large window above the desk allowed the morning sun to stretch across the floor.

Tildano gestured to the counter where there were stacks of the same sort of hard-side cases that had held the cameos, though they varied in width and depth.

"This is where we work with items going in and out of storage," he explained. "I set the case down here while I affixed the cameos inside it, and placed the Holy Father's letter with them."

Holmes placed his hat and cane on the counter and inspected its surface with keen interest. "Where exactly did you set the case?"

"Here." Tildano rested his hands on the countertop, directly in front of the other cases.

The detective took one of the cases down from the stack and laid it in front of Tildano. "Just like this?"

"Yes."

"And you opened it like so?" Holmes flipped the clasp and opened the case in front of the curator.

"Yes."

"Were there any other people around when you did this?"

"No—well, not exactly. I have several assistants and they were working among those shelves."

"Pardon me one moment." He walked behind the nearest shelf, and then returned. "Very good. Now, you say you affixed the cameos inside?"

"Yes, with pins like these—" Tildano went to a metal tray that rested on the counter close to the shelves, and lifted out a small u-shaped pin. "I used these to hold them in place by sticking them into the backing fabric."

"I see. Then you placed His Holiness's note inside, and closed the case."

"Precisely. And I placed a small padlock like this one, over the clasp." He pulled a small lock from the same utility tray that held the pins.

"Were you distracted at all between the time you closed the case and when you put the lock on it?"

"Well—no—wait. Yes. I knocked that utility tray onto the floor."

"You knocked it onto the floor?"

"Yes. It must have caught my sleeve when I picked up the padlock because it slid right off onto the floor. It was quite a mess. My assistants all heard it and came out to help clean up. While they worked, I attached the lock to the case and fastened it."

Suddenly, Holmes picked up the tray Tildano indicated and flipped it over on the counter. All the items in the tray spilled out, scattering all around with some dropping to the floor.

"What on earth—?" said Tildano.

"Wait," I said, holding up my hand. "Let him do what he wills."

Holmes walked to the window and held the tray up in the light. He then removed a magnifying lens from his pocket to examine its edge. "Holiness, would you look at this?"

I went to Holmes' side and squinted through the lens.

"Right here," he said, pointing to the corner. "Do you see the tiny hole?"

I took my reading glasses from my pocket, held them up to my eyes, and looked through lens again. "Yes, I see. There's a loop of sewing thread tied through it."

"Indeed. Grey sewing thread. The perfect colour to match the floor tiling, the countertop, and the tray itself. Congratulations, Your Holiness. This is not a case of the cameos being mislaid, but a genuine theft—and a rather clever one, too."

Holmes turned back to Tildano whose face was pale with shock. "Whoever did this planned it for some time. They probably didn't know what they were going to steal necessarily, they were just waiting for the perfect item. And the cameos were too enticing a target to pass up, especially since they were going to be travelling across the continent. Their disappearance could be blamed on anything other than a theft at the source."

He set the tray back on the counter and gestured to the cases with his lens. "I see that all these have numbered inventory tags, and I assume the numbers correspond to their shelf location in storage?"

"Yes, Signore," said Tildano.

"The case Vicini took to England was so numbered. Scotland Yard insisted on keeping it as evidence." He stuffed his lens back in his pocket and pulled out a small black notebook, which he opened to a page in the middle. "Three thousand, four hundred seventy one."

"All the numbers are cross referenced in the catalogue drawers."

Holmes went to the catalogue, opened a drawer, and flipped through the cards until he reached the number he was seeking. "Three thousand, four hundred seventy one is listed as a small Egyptian figure of Ra."

"We placed that in the Egyptian section two weeks ago."

"The thief switched cases." The detective pushed the drawer shut.

"How is that possible? I was standing right there!"

"As you said, you were distracted by the tray. He was very quick."

"You're not saying it was one of my assistants."

Holmes placed a finger to his lips, then asked in a quiet voice. "There was no one else here, correct?"

"The courier came in from the other room to help," Tildano replied in an equally quiet voice, "as he heard the crash."

Holmes shook his head. "It was not Vicini. How many assistants do you have?"

"Four."

"They are not here now?"

"There was nothing pressing, so when three asked if they could go to smoke, I allowed them. I don't allow smoking in this room or in the workroom since smoke can damage the artwork. There's a room for smoking nearby. I'm not sure if they went there."

"And the other?"

"He doesn't smoke. He said he'd be working in the shelves, but I've not heard him. He's probably still there."

"When did they leave?"

"Quarter of eleven, Signore. Wait—Vernet left earlier, closer to ten thirty—"

"Vernet?" Holmes eyes narrowed.

"Yes, from Paris. A relative of the French artist—"

"Émile Jean-Horace Vernet?"

"You know of him, Signore?"

"He was my great uncle, though I never met him." I could tell that this discovery of a possible relative did not necessarily excite the Englishman. He glanced at his pocket watch. "It's eleven now. That's a lot of time to smoke a cigarette or even two. Did all of them exit through the workroom?"

"I know Vernet did. I'm not sure about the other two. There is another exit at the rear of this room that leads to the Belvedere Courtyard."

"All of your assistants were here on the day you gave what you believed to be the cameo case to the courier?"

"Yes. But wouldn't I notice someone pulling a case from the counter and walking away with it?"

"He didn't walk away with it. He set it with the other cases." Holmes pointed to the stack of cases against the wall.

"Dear God," Tildano whispered.

"As I said, clever. He had you believe you knocked over the tray, when he'd actually hooked it to thread through the shelf there. He watched through the shelf and waited until you'd closed the case and reached to take out a padlock. He then tugged the thread and the entire tray fell off the counter. He rushed around to help, snapping the thread while he did so, and as everyone's attention was engaged, he simply put your case with the others and set one of the empty ones in its place.

"Now, tell me," Holmes continued. "Is there a difference between this stack of cases, and this one here?" He pointed to a second stack next to the first one.

"Those have items in them. They are going back into storage."

"As I suspected." A slight smile appeared his face, and his cool eyes became slits. "He is patient this one. Do you have a log of some sort where you record when items go into storage?"

"Yes. Right here." Tildano went the desk and pulled a journal book from the centre drawer. "The storage case numbers are listed under the date in which they are shelved, so we know what was done on a particular day. If you want to know what the items are, of course, you can look in the catalogue."

Holmes turned the pages to the date in question. "May twenty-second." He went to the catalogue with the book and began flipping through drawers and cards, cross-checking the numbers. "Here it is. Roman cameos, number three thousand nine hundred and forty-three." He pulled the card from the drawer and tucked the log book under his arm. "Shall we look?"

"You really think they are here?" Tildano asked, pointing to the storage shelves.

"I think he put them here himself along with the items set aside to be stored. Where else would he be able to take them from the case freely? He couldn't do it on the counter. Better to remove them in the privacy of the dark storage room shelves where few people go, where one is expected to be seen, and where he could cover his tracks during the searches." He started back into the shelves and we followed him.

"But wouldn't he have removed them by now?" I asked.

"We won't know unless we look, Holiness. As I said, he is patient. He must realise that the cameos are being sought, and he'd wait until the search is called off."

"But this is such an obvious place to look," said Tildano.

"Hiding in plain sight is not unusual. Many thieves use such trickery to throw off suspicion. Ah, here is the aisle." He led us down the walkway between the shelves to the tag number he sought and pulled a case from the shelf. He set it in the curator's hands while he opened the latch.

Inside were a collection of ancient coins.

Holmes closed the case. "He switched the tags and placed the proper case elsewhere. Clever, but not clever enough I'll wager." He took the log book from under his arm while

Tildano placed the case back on the shelf. "He used your system against you, Signore Tildano. But, he must work within that system to remain above notice. Let's check the other numbers shelved that same day. The next one on the list is three thousand nine hundred and sixty-two. That would be the next aisle." He led us around the shelves.

And there we all stopped in surprise. The body of a man lay upon the floor face down, blood pooling around his head.

"Pegrini!" Tildano cried. He went to the body. "He's been bludgeoned to death!"

"Well," said Holmes. "I believe we now know where the cameos were placed." He crouched by the man and felt his neck. "Still quite warm. This happened a very short time ago."

"Lord, have mercy," I whispered. I crossed myself and prayed for the repose of his soul.

"I did say that if we surprised him the thief may make a mistake. I believe this is it."

"This is more than a mistake, Signore," I said. "This is an abomination!"

"I agree, Your Holiness," Holmes said. Removing the magnifying lens from his pocket once more, he inspected the wound on the back of the man's head. "What man does to man in the interest of greed is shocking." Holmes' face rose from the body, and he sniffed the air.

"What is it, Signore?" I asked.

"He doesn't smoke," Holmes muttered to no one in particular. He went back to examining the body.

I turned to the captain of the guard, who'd followed us into the storage room. "Go find a priest, quickly. Tell him I wish him to bring the oil of anointing. And summon the other guards."

"You would give someone Last Rites after death, Holiness?" asked Holmes, looking up at me.

"With the Sacrament of Extreme Unction, the body of a Christian may be anointed after death until corruption occurs for we only know the soul has left the body at that point. Since he has not reached rigor, he may be anointed."

"Interesting," said Holmes. "I was unaware of that." He tapped his temple with the magnifying lens. "It is a fact I shall keep in my mental repertoire." He returned his attention to the dead man. "This is the assistant who did not go out this morning."

"Yes," said Tildano.

"And yet he seems to have found a small friend." He moved the young man's left hand an inch to the left. "One of your 'messengers,' Holiness." Lying next to his thumb was a dead, yellow-white honeybee.

"He was out in the gardens?"

"No, I believe our killer and thief was and managed to bother our buzzing compatriots. The dead bee must have clung to his clothing."

"Wouldn't we have seen him out in the garden?"

"We were distracted, were we not?"

I released a deep sigh. My attack of angina had turned our attention away from the brigand.

With his magnifying lens, Holmes crawled along the body, inspecting the floor as he made his way around to the man's feet. At one point he stopped and picked up something I did not see, analyzing it under the lens. He placed whatever it was in a small white envelope he pulled from his inside breast pocket. He then turned his attention to the man's shoes.

"What prompts a man to murder another in cold blood?" I murmured. "It has always confounded me."

"In this case, desperation. It was premeditated but not much time was taken in the planning because our killer was careless about it." Holmes turned on his knees to the shelves that were at his eye level with his lens, focusing on the storage cases. After examining the edge of one, he tapped it with his finger. "This is the murder weapon. There is blood on the corner. He hit Signore Pegrini with it from behind and crushed in his skull."

Holmes stood, stuffed the envelope into his right pocket, and opened the log book he had under his arm, checking the numbers again. He then pulled a case from the shelf at his elbow. He handed it to Tildano and opened it. Lying on the velvet was Our letter to Victoria and nothing else. Holmes lifted it from the box and held it up.

"I would like to meet your assistants, Signore Tildano," Holmes said, dropping the letter back in the empty case.

"Of course, Signore. But I find the whole possibility of their guilt disturbing. All of them came here with excellent recommendations."

"I'm sure they did. Which one has been employed here the longest?"

"Pegrini," he said, nodding to the unfortunate victim. "He's been here three years."

"And the second longest?"

"Signore Fiore and Signore Rossini were employed at almost the same time, nearly six months ago. They were the two who left together."

"And the last was Vernet?"

Tildano nodded. "Signore Vernet came to us from the Louvre two months ago."

Just then the lieutenant returned with the priest who carried a sick call case containing the holy oil I'd requested. It was a priest I knew, Bernard O'Reilly. He was a prothonotary, a devout, intelligent man whom the year before I'd given leave to write my biography in English from my personal memoirs. O'Reilly was a balding, bespectacled, man of later years who looked pale and grim when he saw the horror on the floor in front of him.

I acknowledged his presence to turn his attention from the gruesome scene. "Grazie for coming, Father O'Reilly. It's good to see you."

"Thank you, Holy Father," he handed me his sick case, then genuflected to kiss my ring with a nervous wobble. "I wish it were for a better circumstance. I was just doing some work in the Apostolic Library when your soldiers told me of this tragedy." His Italian was tinged with the flatter vowels of an American and a hint of an Irish lilt, a trait which I'd always found charming.

"Signore Holmes, you don't mind—?" I gestured to the young man on the floor.

"Not at all. While you see to that, I would like to visit the Belvedere Courtyard if I may?"

"Surely, Signore," said Tildano. "It's right out this way." Tildano showed him the way into the shelves, and then returned alone a moment later.

I placed my cappello and cane on the shelf along with O'Reilly's case. From the case I removed the purple stole, which I kissed and placed around my neck. Taking the tiny container of *Oleum Infirmorum*, I said, "Assist me, please, Father." O'Reilly grasped my arm to help me kneel on the floor next to the body and bent down beside me along with Tildano to help me turn the young man over onto his back. The victim was a handsome young man with an innocent round face. That one so young would meet so violent an end grieved me all the more.

As I opened the small jar of oil, the light, oddly familiar smell of something akin to incense tickled my nose—a smell that was certainly not the oil, which is made from olives. I brushed the thought of it aside, thinking it to be merely one of those strange smells old buildings often have. Touching the oil upon my fingertips, I proceeded with my task.

"Through this Holy Unction," I said softly, in Latin, using the longer version of the anointing rite—for the poor young man deserved that much, "and through the great goodness of His mercy, may God pardon thee whatever sins thou hast committed by evil use of sight." I closed the man's open, glaring green eyes, tracing oil upon their lids. I then repeated these words for hearing while touching his ears, for smell while touching his nostrils, for taste and speech, his lips, for touch, his hands, and for the ability to walk, his feet. My heart grew heavier as I anointed each of the man's senses, for I made a most horrible realisation.

His death was my fault.

I had brought all of this upon him through offering an audacious gift to Victoria. Was it worth it? Victoria's suspicious gaze from the distant past melded in my mind with John Henry Newman's tearful one, and this young man's glassy dead one.

Blinking away a mist in my own eyes, I marked a cross upon the young man's forehead with my thumb and whispered, "We impart upon you Our Apostolic blessing and grant you a plenary indulgence for the remission of all your sins, and We bless you." I made the sign of the cross over him. "*In nomine Patris, et Filii, et Spiritus Sancti. Amen.*"

I sensed movement to my right, and turned my head to see that Holmes had returned and was crouching next to me. He glanced at my hand. Looking down I saw that the young man's blood was on my fingertips.

"We must do right by him," I said.

I meant my own person in the royal "We," but he took my statement to mean us together. "And so we shall," he replied. He pulled a handkerchief from his inside breast pocket and offered it to me.

"Signore, if I use that to wipe my hand, it will have the holy oil upon it, and it will have to be burned."

"That is all right, Holiness. I have another."

"*Grazie.*" I took his offered handkerchief to wipe my fingers, and he helped me stand. I stuffed the handkerchief in my pocket, removed the stole, and placed it and the oil back in O'Reilly's case. "*Grazie* again, Father O'Reilly, for coming so quickly," I said.

"I'm happy to be of service, Holy Father."

Over my brother priest's shoulder I noticed three young men peering around the shelves with the captain of the guard and his fellows—Tildano's assistants, no doubt. The three appeared shocked at the scene before them.

I was not convinced by their display.

"Signori," I greeted them with asperity. "How good of you to join us."

Realizing they'd caught my attention, they went to their knees. I decided to let them remain there as I closed O'Reilly's case, handed it to him, and turned to my English friend. "I believe you have some business with these gentlemen, Signore?"

"Yes. Signore Tildano, may we use your office?"

"Certainly, Signore."

"Is there anything more you need to see with regard to Signore Pegrini?" I asked Holmes, gesturing to the victim.

"I've seen all there is, Holiness."

"*Va bene.*" I took my cappello and walking stick from the shelf. "Signore Tildano, you should notify the infirmary morgue so this young man can be properly cared for."

"Yes, Holy Father," said Tildano.

"Captain," I said turning to the soldiers. "Please show these young men to the curator's office." I directed them away with tip of my walking stick.

Holmes moved to follow the soldiers but I stopped him by with a light touch on his arm. "Do you want me present while you question them, Signore? I do not wish to be a hindrance."

"Holiness, your air of intimidation would be a boon during this interview."

"I think I can manage intimidation quite well."

"Excellent. Pray, after you." He held out his hand for me to precede him.

"No, after you, Signore. I must make a sufficiently regal entrance, no?"

"Indeed you must." He walked ahead of me back through the shelves and gathered up his hat and walking stick from the counter as we proceeded to Tildano's office.

I entered after the guards took up a position outside the door. The young men were milling about the office. Holmes, having preceded me, had placed his hat and cane on Tildano's desk, and now leaned his lanky frame against it in a casual pose. I tapped my walking stick hard on the wooden floor to get the assistants' attention. All three of the young men scrambled to drop to their knees in a row. Pacing in front of them with my hand behind my back, I studied them as a general reviewing the troops. "Signori," I said, stopping to stand next to Holmes. "As you no doubt noticed, there was a peculiar incident this morning."

"But, Holiness, we were not here." A moustached young man on the end started.

"Did We give you leave to speak, young man?"

"N-no."

"What is your name?"

"Rossini, Holy Father."

97

"Signore Rossini, you are to remain silent until We address you."

"Yes, Holy Father." He dropped his eyes to the floor.

"This gentleman with me is Sherlock Holmes. He will be asking you questions. You will answer all of them truthfully and show him proper respect. Is this understood?"

They all nodded, though the young man on the opposite end, a thin youth with a sharp nose and blue eyes, looked troubled. "Sherlock Holmes," he muttered.

"Is there a problem, young man?" I asked.

His face paled in surprise at my addressing him. "No, Holy Father," he answered in what was clearly a French accent. "It is simply that I understand Monsieur Holmes and I may have some relation to each other."

"Horace Vernet," Holmes said.

The young man nodded. "He was my great-grandfather, though I feel you look more like him than I do."

"What is your full name?" Holmes asked.

"Jean Phillipe Vernet-Delrouche. Horace Vernet's daughter Louise was my grandmother."

"And you go by her surname. Why?"

The young man's expression was sheepish. "It's easier to spell and say, especially for those with whom I work who do not speak French."

I was impressed at this. That others would have difficulty with French is usually not the concern of a Frenchman. The young man clearly had a sensitive nature.

"I understand you came here from the Louvre," Holmes said.

"Yes, Monsieur."

"Was your position not satisfactory there?"

"It was more than satisfactory, Monsieur."

"Then why did you come here?"

The young man hesitated and looked at his two fellow assistants who were gazing at him with curiosity.

"I'd rather not say," he replied in a quiet voice.

"I'm afraid you have no choice," said Holmes. "His Holiness was clear that you were to answer my questions, was he not?"

"Yes, of course." He released a hopeless sigh. "I came to Rome because I thought I might have a calling to the priesthood. I thought if I were here in Rome itself, the answer to this question might be more apparent to me one way or the other."

Holmes raised his eyebrows. This was clearly not the answer he was expecting. "You were going to discover this from handling artwork and antiquities?"

"Well, I—"

"Never mind, that is neither here nor there. Where did you go this morning?"

"I went out to have a cigarette."

"It only takes three to five minutes to smoke a cigarette. You were gone nearly forty-five minutes."

"I—" He glanced over at me nervously and dropped his gaze to the floor.

"What is it that you hesitate to say, Monsieur?" Holmes prompted. "Surely His Holiness has heard worse in the confessional?"

"I went to meet a woman." He said it quickly and looked at me to gauge my reaction. I said nothing, but tapped my index finger on the top of my walking stick, expectant of an explanation.

"What of the priesthood?" Holmes asked.

"That's the point. I met her when I first arrived in Rome, but while she's a pleasant young woman I realised that I could not continue with her if I were truly to decide my future. We'd always meet at the Four Gates at the other end of the museum with her chaperone. So I'd made an appointment with her there this morning to break it off."

"And did you?"

"Yes."

Holmes took a sheet of paper from the desk and motioned for the young man to stand. "Write her name on this paper with her address."

"But—"

Holmes tapped the paper impatiently.

Vernet came to the desk, dipped a pen in the inkwell and scribbled down the information for Holmes.

Taking the paper from the young man, Holmes folded it and

put it in his breast pocket. "Excellent. Now, might I trouble you for one of your cigarettes? I smoked my last just before I arrived and I've been without tobacco all morning."

"Oh—uh—certainly." Vernet pulled his cigarette case from his breast pocket and offered its contents to Holmes.

"Thank you," the Englishman said. He took one cigarette and tapped it on his palm. "Holiness, you don't mind if I—?"

"Not at all, Signore."

He sniffed the cigarette. "Am I mistaken or is this Gaulois tobacco?"

Vernet nodded. "It is."

"A tobacco of a rather intense flavour. I've always liked it. I suppose you found a decent tobacconist nearby?" Holmes removed a small box of matches from his left pocket and lit the cigarette.

"Rossini and Fiore recommended one to me when I started here," Vernet said. "Bianchini Rivéndita —"

"On the Borgo Pio," I finished for him.

Holmes turned to me. "You know it, Holiness?"

"That is the store from which Monsignor Macchi orders my snuff. I used to buy it there myself when I was a cardinal."

"I see the shop comes highly recommended! I shall seek it out post-haste. I am, in fact, quite partial to clove tobacco."

"I don't prefer that myself, Monsieur," said Vernet. "But they do have a good selection of clove tobacco there. In fact, I believe that is Monsieur Fiore's choice."

At the mention of his name, Fiore, the third assistant who'd remained silent during the entire interview, lifted his gaze from the floor. He was a sturdily built man in his late twenties or early thirties with a tawny, Southern Italian complexion and hooked nose. His black eyes studied the Frenchman with a strangely severe gaze.

"Really?" said Holmes. "Is this so, Signore Fiore?"

Fiore's frown curled into a polite smile. "Yes, Signore."

"Capital. I look forward to trying their products." He gave them an impatient wave. "And with that, I'll call the end of this interview. Thank you for coming, Signori."

The three assistants looked at each other quizzically, then to me. I shooed them with my fingers, and the two on the floor stood to leave with their French co-worker.

Holmes called out, "Oh, Signore Fiore."

The young man turned back.

"For the bee sting on your right hand, I recommend a paste of bicarbonate of soda with a little water. It will relieve the irritation."

Fiore's dark eyes widened. "Thank you, Signore," he said, and left.

Holmes went to the door to close it behind him, then spun back to face me with a glint in his steely eyes.

"It is Fiore, isn't it?" I asked.

"Not he alone, Holiness," he said, waving his index finger in the air as he paced back to me. "He and his friend Rossini together. They went out together, they came back together. And having an assistant in this is advantageous as one covers the other. It certainly made their diversion for the theft more seamless."

"But what was this with Vernet and the tobacco?"

"When I knelt near Pegrini's body, I smelled a clove cigarette. The scent of clove tobacco is quite distinctive and will often linger after the smoker leaves, even if the cigarette was not smoked at that location. Therefore, someone had been nearby that recently smoked one— and we know that Pegrini did not smoke."

"Come to think of it, I smelled something odd myself, but I didn't know what it was."

"That is why I'm here, Holiness," Holmes replied. "I also found, near the body, bits of fine, red gravel. This, of course, in an area with very little foot traffic that looked to have been swept recently. In checking Pegrini's shoes, I knew the gravel was not from him, for these sorts of pebbles tend to get stuck in and around one's soles, and there were none there.

"I therefore walked out to the Belvedere Courtyard and found that it is freshly lined with this very gravel. I also discovered that across the courtyard is an entrance to a short hall through the building that leads back out onto the garden path on the other side."

"The door by the bee hive."

"Precisely. It is there that I found these." From the left pocket of his coat he produced a small white envelope from which he dropped two cigarette ends onto the palm of his hand. "Clove cigarettes. His compatriot had also smoked one, offered to him by his friend, no doubt. I saw these on our way in, actually, but I thought nothing of them until I smelled the clove around Pegrini's body. Of course, when I entered this room, the scent of clove was here. And as we now know," he held up the cigarette in his right hand that he'd almost spent himself, "Vernet does not smoke clove cigarettes. That and his willingness to offer an alibi at great discomfort to himself, eliminates him from suspicion.

"Also," he continued, returning the cigarette remains to his pocket, "as these gentlemen were kneeling—part of the reason I wanted your presence here, Holiness, how useful that position can be!—I saw that Rossini and Fiore had the Belvedere Courtyard gravel stuck in the soles of their shoes. It was not deeply embedded, which meant it was very recently trod upon. There was also garden soil on their shoes, giving further confirmation of where they'd been."

I shook my head and smiled. "You are impressive, young man."

"Thank you, Holiness."

"The one thing we still do not know, however," I said, "is where the cameos are now. I assume they must have hid them again while they were out, as they'd surely not wish to be searched upon their return."

"You know the criminal mind well, Your Holiness."

"My first position as a priest was to deal with lawlessness in Benevento. I became quite familiar the habits of thieves and murderers."

"Then you know that thieves often steal from other thieves."

"Yes, there is 'no honour among thieves,' as the saying goes. Thievery is mortally sinful and one such sin builds upon another."

"But what if one who is just steals from a thief to return items to their rightful owner?" Holmes took one last puff of the cigarette and squashed out the remains of it in Tildano's desk ashtray. He gazed at me expectantly as he exhaled smoke from his lips.

"That is a different case, of course. The person would be justified in returning stolen property."

"Ah, that sets my mind at ease. I was thinking you'd have me repent."

"Signore?"

A wide, bright smile spread across Holmes' lean face. He reached into his right pocket and removed his spare, clean handkerchief and unfolded it before my eyes.

There, resting in the pristine white linen, lay the precious cameos.

"Signore!" I cried, grasping his arm in surprise. "Where on earth—?"

"*In* earth, rather, Holiness. I found them precisely where I thought I would when I discovered the clove cigarettes."

"Where?"

"In the hole left by the removed hedge directly next to the bee hive. They were wrapped in another handkerchief under some garden soil. Our culprits thought the bees would keep everyone away until they could come back for them. But kicking dirt over their plunder irritated our insect friends and caused Fiore to be stung."

"Marvellous. I will have these men detained."

"Not yet, Holiness."

"No? Why?"

"We need them to return for their ill gotten gains, and we must catch them red-handed. That would solidify the case against them."

He was right—while we had courts in the Vatican, we had no prisons and had to rely on Italy for that service, paying a hostile government for the expense of incarceration. More often than not, even with our paid tribute, they were not entirely accommodating unless the culprit was truly dangerous to their citizenry.

"Of course the thieves will realise the cameos are not where they left them," I said.

"Not immediately. They'll find a parcel of equal weight to pull from the ground, giving us adequate time to witness their actions. I substituted the cameos in their parcel with something else, which, if I may say so, is equally precious to their owner."

"What would that be?"

Holmes pulled a bronze coin from his watch pocket and placed it in my hand. It was a coin minted for my jubilee the previous year, bearing my own profile on one side and my coat of arms on the other.

"We met your elderly gardener Antonio outside. He had a small handful of these in his pocket. He apparently treasures them, but he was willing to part with them for our little ruse. His ten-year old grandson, meanwhile, agreed to watch the spot from a hidden location and inform us if he sees our thieves return."

I chuckled, flipping the coin over in my palm. "I must admit, I thought I'd never hear of this until my funeral."

"What do you mean, Holiness?"

"That We would be the Vicar of Christ *in* earth rather than *on* it."

Holmes laughed. "Holiness, you are a joy."

Just then, there was a heavy knock at the door. Holmes folded the handkerchief quickly over the cameos and put them back in his pocket as he strode across the room to open the door.

The captain of the guard stood at the threshold. "Holy Father, there's a boy here who—"

A very agitated young boy pushed around him. "My grandfather, Signore!" he cried. "They've taken him!"

"What? Where?" asked Holmes.

"To his tool shed behind the Holy Father's palazzina. They took him there because they only found the coins, not what they buried. They said he stole their things—"

"Captain," I said to guardsman. "Take two men and go there quickly. Signore Holmes, go with them. I will catch up to you. Young man," I said to the boy, whose large brown eyes were wide at my speaking to him. "You stay here."

Holmes snatched up his hat and stick, and rushed out ahead

of me with the soldiers. I followed them at a pace that would not upset my constitution with one remaining halberdier. After exiting the door we'd entered originally, I lost sight of them as they passed the Casino of Pius V due west from the museum. I followed along the same path, walking around the south side of the Fountain of the Eagle with the Leonine wall to my left and peered around a bend in that 9th century fortification to look upon the temporary wooden garden shed abutting it. As I reached this spot, the bells of the noon Angelus began to toll at St. Peter's. But the devotion could have to come later, for the alarming situation that met my eyes beyond my hiding place arrested my attention.

Fiore's left arm pinioned the old gardener at his throat, and with his opposite hand, he held a handgun to the man's head. My soldiers had encircled him along with Holmes, whose walking stick rested at his feet—dropped, I assumed, at the command of the gunman. Holmes' back was closest to me. A figure whom I believed to be Fiore's compatriot Rossini lay crumpled on the ground near the wall. A halberdier stood over him holding his pole arm like a quarterstaff—the soldier had apparently brought him low with a blow to his belly.

"He has a gun," my halberdier said of Fiore. His broad body moved in front of mine as a shield.

"Yes, and there is something important you must do right now, my son." He turned to me with wide eyes. I whispered specific instructions to him and as I spoke he shook his head in protest.

"I cannot leave you, Holy Father."

"You must. Do as I say and trust in God. Be ready. You'll know when to act. Go, now."

The soldier frowned, uncertain, but he had to obey. As he ran back past the fountain, I crossed myself and prayed for Saint Michael's protection. Setting my walking stick against the ancient wall, I stepped out of my hiding place to stand to the right of the Englishman.

"Holiness," Holmes murmured to me. "You should not be here."

"I know, Signore," I replied, wishing among all wishes I could do as he suggested. "Please, may I have the cameos?"

"What?" He peered at me from the corner of his eyes.

"I have need of them."

Holmes slowly moved his right hand to reach into his coat pocket.

"Signore Holmes," cried Fiore. "Keep your hands from your pockets or I'll pull the trigger."

"He is merely giving me what you want, young man," I said. "That is all."

"He has the cameos?"

"Yes."

Fiore pressed the gun harder against his prisoner's temple. "Do it quickly," he ordered through his teeth.

The old gardener groaned.

"Please, my son. Do not harm him. You've already killed one innocent man. Do not multiply your grievous offences to Our Lord by murdering another."

"I want the cameos and I want to walk away."

"And you shall," I promised. Holmes now held out his handkerchief to me. The fingers of my left hand trembled as I took it from him. I reached out with my other hand and peeled the fabric open in my palm. "See?" I held the cameos low so Fiore could view them. "They are all here. Pray, let the man go. I will place these in your hand, and you may walk away."

Fiore's black eyes studied all those surrounding him, considering my offer. "Why should I believe you?" he asked me.

"I am the successor of Peter, and I give you my solemn word. One life is enough, young man. Please. Take the cameos and go."

Fiore flung the old man roughly aside and aimed the gun at my chest. His free left hand was now outstretched, waiting for the cameos.

"Stop!" I cried, holding up my empty hand to the soldiers, for I could see they were ready to pounce or fire depending on which weapon they were carrying. "Hold. Do nothing to him."

"Holy Father—" my captain protested.

"I will not lose another, not even him. Now, hold your

peace." Taking a deep breath, I walked forward with the cameos gripped tightly in my fist. My heart pounded heavily in my chest. I placed the small bundle solidly in the thief's outstretched palm, the barrel of his pistol only an inch from my pectoral cross. "Go, now." I pointed over his shoulder.

He glanced around once more at my soldiers who were held at my word, then turned to run to his rear. Suddenly the halberdier whom I'd sent through my palazzina to the other side of the shed, leaped out of his hiding place, swinging his blade from front to back to hook the young man's ankle. Fiore fell flat on his face and his weapon tumbled away in the grass. The halberdier

I PLACED THE SMALL BUNDLE SOLIDLY IN THE THIEF'S OUTSTRETCHED PALM.

then continued the swing of his axe up and back down, and in one movement plunged the top pike into the shoulder fabric of Fiore's coat, twisting the handle of the weapon. The blade of the hatchet now rested at Fiore's neck, and he was pinned to the ground. Blood seeped through the fabric of his jacket, his left shoulder apparently nicked by the sharp edge of the pike.

Next to me, Holmes said, "They really can use those things. I wonder if the Yeomen of the Guard are as skilful."

"Please, Signore. Do not say you thought they were merely ornaments."

Looking to my left, I noticed the shocked gardener still on his knees in the grass. I went to him and held out my hand. "Are you all right?"

He grasped my hand and kissed it with trembling lips. "Holy Father, you saved me. How do I repay you?"

I gripped his elbow and helped him to stand. He seemed nearly my own age, though I determined the wrinkles of his face to be more from the sun than of so numerous of years. "Make the gardens beautiful as you always have," I said. "We'll be moving to Our palazzina for the summer next week and We look forward to enjoying them."

"With pleasure, Holy Father."

I then turned my attention to the restrained man who was sputtering and growling a few steps away, still pinned to the turf.

"You lied! You gave me your solemn word as pope!" he snarled. "You said I could walk away."

"And you *did*, my son," I said. "About eight paces. But I certainly was not going to allow more than that."

Holmes picked up the linen bundle Fiore had dropped and placed it in my hand. "I never would have expected you to do that, Holiness."

"I did not expect it either." With a deep sigh, I placed the cameos in my pocket with my spectacles, then spoke to all present. "As the signore is now incapacitated and the bells did sound a few moments ago, we will pray the Angelus and give thanks."

Making the sign of the cross, I led all present in the devotion, and unexpectedly, from Holmes at my elbow, I heard some murmured responses in English. As I finished with the sign of the cross, I saw him doing the same. He shrugged to me and said, "When in Rome—"

"Holy Father!" It was Rossini who'd regained consciousness while the guard bound his hands. "Holy Father, please, I wish to confess."

"The second thief is repentant," mused Holmes. "How biblical."

I smiled. I was heartened by Rossini's expression of repentance. The soldiers who had finished binding him grappled him more roughly as I stepped closer to him, but I shook my head to them.

"What do you wish to confess, my son?" I asked, placing my hand on his shoulder.

"Everything, Holy Father. I'll tell you whatever you want to know, about me, about *him*." His lips curled in a disgusted scowl as he nodded his head to Fiore.

"This should be interesting to hear," said Holmes, crossing his arms.

"Do you always listen to confessions, Signore?" I asked.

"I've heard my share," he replied. "Though I admit I do not pronounce an absolution when I do."

"I'm glad of that." I turned back to Rossini. "Do you wish your confession to be public or private?"

"Holiness, I would shout it from the hilltop!"

"Very well then," I said, swinging my hand from my body in a wide gesture. "As we are on a Roman hilltop, please shout away."

"You talk and you will die, Rossini, as will your family." Fiore snarled, as the guards bound him.

"I might as well be dead anyway and my family too, for prison will surely cause them to starve." Rossini gazed up at me with eyes full of desperation. "Holy Father, this man is—"

"—Enrico Falcone. The notorious art thief."

Rossini gaped at Holmes. "Yes, how did you know?"

"I wasn't entirely sure until I saw his gun. It's a Mauser 1878 7.6 millimetre solid frame Zig-Zag revolver, a unique model that Falcone used in his several murderous thefts in London. I suspected it was he when I encountered the clove cigarettes." Holmes turned Fiore. "You recognised me in the garden, didn't you? That's why you hurried to take the cameos and killed Pegrini in the process?"

Fiore, or rather, Falcone, only sneered.

"Scotland Yard would be happy to have their hands on you should His Holiness wish to extradite you." Holmes' eyes flashed to me with satisfaction. "I helped Scotland Yard completely dismantle his art thieving ring in England, but I daresay he escaped the net. I never saw his face, so clever was he. He is quite good at disguise and an excellent forger—his copies were works of art in themselves. He also can forge documents, which accounts for his references. I would have Signore Tildano conduct a thorough inventory, for some of the museum's art is bound to be missing or replaced with fakes."

"I know what he took for the most part," volunteered Rossini. "I'd be happy to tell you."

"How did you come to be with him?" asked Holmes. "You don't seem too admiring of your friend."

"He's no friend." Rossini glared at the other thief. "I admit, when I was quite young, I helped him in his early escapades. When he left Italy, I finished my schooling and found myself a wife. I wanted no more of his world. But when he returned, he hunted me down and compelled me to apply for one of two open positions at the Vatican Museum, using my then stainless reputation to continue his thievery. He held the lives of my wife and child over my head. He was desperate for help since his band was all captured in London." Rossini shook his head. "Pegrini didn't deserve to die. I saw Falcone bash his head in. And I would be happy to testify to that. But because I helped Falcone steal, I'll serve my sentence."

"An excellent confession, don't you agree Signore Holmes?" I raised an eyebrow at my friend.

"I found it more than satisfactory, Holiness."

"My son, you will remain in the guard house until we can try you. It should not be long. We believe Our court can be lenient because of your frankness."

"Will you not grant me absolution, Holy Father?" Rossini asked.

"Ah, so you really *do* want that?"

"I do."

"*Va bene.*" I spoke the absolution and blessed him. "For your penance you may pray the rosary today, but you must also serve your sentence. Do you have a rosary?"

"No, I don't, Holy Father."

"We will have one brought to you. And We will ask Signore Tildano about your family, to see how We may help them."

"Thank you, Holy Father."

"Now, you." I turned to the other thief. "Have you any regret for what you've done?"

"I am only sorry I didn't shoot you."

I nodded. "I understand."

He lifted his chin and glared at me, his angry eyes boring into my own. "What could you possibly understand?"

"More than you realise," I said. "You are frustrated. No matter what you take, it's never enough. You steal more and even kill for it. But none of it satisfies you. And I am yet another galling hindrance to your goal of happiness."

Falcone grimaced. He turned his gaze to the ground.

"But I am glad you did not shoot me," I continued, "for I believe Our soldiers would have killed you in return. As it is, you now you have time—time to consider what it is you've been seeking. We will contact the British Embassy and Scotland Yard about sending you to England, though I fear it may mean the gallows."

"No doubt," said Holmes.

"While justice must be served, We will request your life be spared. We will also ask Cardinal Manning to make certain a priest is readily available to you."

As the guards lead the two away, I turned to Holmes, who waited nearby with one hand on his walking stick, the other behind his back. His eyes followed me with a studying gaze as I retrieved my own walking stick. "Are you hungry for luncheon, Signore?" I asked him.

"Lunch sounds excellent," he admitted. Together we headed

toward the palace across the gardens which were now in bloom. A single halberdier, the same who'd pinioned the culprit, stepped ahead of us to lead the way though the sculptured green paths. "I could really smoke a pipe about now, though," he said. "I wasn't lying when I said I'd exhausted all of my tobacco on the trip here. In my haste to leave, I apparently forgot my extra pouch."

"I have an adequate selection of tobacco in my apartments, Signore. I do not smoke, but I often have guests who do. You may have all you wish."

Holmes seemed relieved. "You are most generous, Holiness."

"I am a servant of the servants of God, my son," I said, bowing with my head. "Though I am not sure I have clove tobacco."

"That's all right, Holiness," he said with a wide grin. "I personally find it to be the most vile substance on Earth."

I laughed. "Signore, you amaze me."

"And you, Holiness, have certainly amazed me."

"Yes, well." I smiled. "Sometimes I amaze myself."

ITE, MISSA EST

After Signore Holmes shared a pleasant luncheon with me, Pio supplied him with several choices of tobacco. He then went to find his French relative to request a personal tour of the museum while I took a much needed siesta. When I woke, I met with members of the Curia, composed a new letter to Victoria for the cameos, and wrote a letter of condolence to the family of the murdered museum employee. That evening, at my invitation, Holmes joined me for dinner and a short concert in the reception room, as vocalists from the Opera della Scala performed selections from their Spring season. He then retired after his busy day. I went to bed early myself, but being unable to sleep as usual, I spent much of the night working on the encyclical, finally nodding off with the pen in my hand in the early hours of morning. I was awakened at my desk by Pio at six thirty to prepare for Mass.

By the time I washed, changed, and vested for Mass it was

seven thirty. It was the feast day of St. Mary Magdalene, and I offered the Holy Sacrifice that day for Signora Murray and her child as I promised, with an additional offering of thanksgiving for Holmes' assistance and prayers for all those involved in this case including the criminals for they were in the most need of mercy. Several of the papal staff were present along with a number of the Swiss Guard. After reading the Gospel, I glanced up before beginning my homily to see the Englishman sitting in the rear pew of the chapel. His eyes were closed and I hoped he was not sleeping, considering it was early in the morning. Then I remembered how he'd sat with his eyes closed with a dreamy expression on his face during the concert the night before, and decided he might be simply listening. So I proceeded with the Mass with the same joy I do every day, and I didn't notice him again for the rest of the liturgy.

After removing my vestments in the sacristy, I returned to the chapel to pray the Hours and the rosary, and spend more time in private contemplation in the Lord's presence. This was my happiest period of day (second only to celebrating Mass), and usually time slipped away from me. It wasn't until Monsignor Macchi touched me on the arm that I realised that nearly an hour had passed.

As I left, I found Holmes in the sitting room outside the chapel smoking a briar pipe with newspapers scattered around him. A new pouch of tobacco lay in his lap.

"Signore, I am very sorry. Have I kept you waiting for me all this time?" I asked.

He looked up from his reading. "Do not apologise, Holiness. You were doing what you should be doing."

"But you want to be on you way, and I have only delayed you."

He shrugged and glanced at his pocket watch. "The train that I must take doesn't leave for another two hours."

"Were you looking for something in particular?" I gestured to the newspapers.

He sighed irritably and started to fold papers together. "While I was out yesterday I couldn't for the life of me find a decent paper to read news of interest from England. It appears that I must wait until I go to the train station."

"I see you've acquired some tobacco, however."

"Yes. I visited the shop you and my cousin recommended. I chose one of the tobaccos your chamberlain favoured me with yesterday. I quite like it."

"Do you wish to have breakfast?"

"I thought you'd never ask."

We shared café latte and rolls in the breakfast room next to the chapel, then he escorted me to my study, where the young, solemn Secretary of State Cardinal Rampolla awaited us.

"Ah, Your Eminence, have you been waiting long?"

"Not at all, Holy Father," he replied.

"You remember Signore Holmes from the concert last night?"

"I do indeed."

"The cameos?" I pointed to the very familiar black case on my desk.

Rampolla nodded. "The Museum curator was here. He affixed them in the case for you so they might be transported."

"He could not wait?"

"He apologised, Holy Father. He said he had to meet with the murdered man's family."

"Ah, yes. Did he take Our letter to them?"

"Yes, Holiness."

"*Va bene.* Shall we make sure they are truly here?" I flipped open the clasp and opened the case to view the contents. The seven cameos were laid out again neatly on the velvet, fixed in place with the special pins. I turned the case so Rampolla and Holmes could both see.

"They are really there, no?"

"Yes, Holiness," they said together.

"I want to be certain I'm not hallucinating." I took Our new letter to Victoria from the desk and placed it in the case, then closed and locked it with the padlock. I handed the key to Holmes and he put it in his watch pocket. "Now," I said. "Before you take this case and return to your beloved queen and country, there is the matter of your compensation."

"The British Government will be compensating me, Holiness."

"Tell them to keep their money. This was intended to be a gift from Us in the first place, so We will take care of the rest. Would five thousand pounds be acceptable to you?"

"Five thousa—" Holmes eyes widened. "That's far too generous, Holiness."

"It is my own money. Being a son of a count gave me that advantage, and the money is going to the Church anyway. We're already renovating the Vatican observatory, so one could consider this payment to you another gift to science. We will have a cheque drawn on Our bank in England. Where should it be sent?"

"The Capital and Counties Bank, Oxford Street branch are my agents—but you must realise it wasn't that difficult of a matter."

"For you." I raised my eyebrows at him.

"Well, yes, but—"

"It is for your special talents and for your willingness to travel three days to solve this problem in a single morning that We reward you. Though I assure you, this case was more complex than it appeared."

"How so?"

"Surely you must have realised that this wasn't merely about missing artwork."

Holmes' penetrating eyes glanced over at my chess set, and his expression cooled. "Of course, I should have known."

"Known what?"

"Chess. It is a sign of a scheming mind."

Rompalla straightened his back with indignation. "Scheming? You insult His Holiness!"

"Peace, Eminence." I held up a hand to my fellow bishop, then said to Holmes, "In Our role as pontiff, We must often play politics. I am trained as a diplomat and it is something I do very well. So I am a tactician, yes. I used that talent in the garden yesterday with Signore Falcone, and I use it now with Victoria. But if I scheme, Signore, I do it not for myself, or my personal glory." I rested my hand on the cameo case. "These cameos are not about me or how they will benefit me, but about how they will benefit the children of God in your country. These cameos are about a *cathedral*."

"A cathedral?" Holmes repeated, his eyes narrowing.

"Yes, a cathedral. In Westminster."

"But there is no cathedral in—" He hesitated, a light dawning in his eyes. "You want to build one."

I nodded. "We have purchased land that was once a prison there. Do you know where I mean?"

"Totill Fields Prison. Yes, I know it."

"While the property is ours we cannot build upon it for the resistance we've encountered from members of your parliament. We hoped a more a true friendship with Victoria would open a path to this end. England has become more favourable to Catholics, Signore. She allows us to celebrate Mass in public now, to have priests and now bishops. Our churches are no longer regularly desecrated by vandals. But to have a bishop's seat, a place to which all English Catholics may look for guidance, a place they can identify as a spiritual home—surely you must realise what it would mean to them."

"Do you really think those cameos would sway Victoria to grant your wish?" Holmes asked.

"It is worth a try."

Holmes frowned. "It seems so trivial."

"Politics, like detection, often deals in trivialities, no?"

"Yes, well, that is true. But you are taking a great chance in telling me these things. How do you know I won't reveal it all to Her Majesty?"

"When you first arrived here you asked me if I valued honesty. I believe you asked not because you wanted to know if I did, but because *you* did. So I am honest with you and tell you all. You are a forthright man. You are a trickster—" I held up my index finger and grinned. "—and a clever tactician in your own right. But you are noble. And for this reason I have faith in you."

"I am honoured you'd say so, Holiness. And I must admit—" He peered at me. "You are truly not what I expected."

"Really? What did you expect?"

"I hesitate to say."

"Oh, I think I know. You anticipated a spoiled, self-righteous, Church nobleman seeking his lost baubles."

Holmes pursed his lips. "Well—"

"That is more descriptive of His Eminence than me." I smiled.

"Holy Father!" Rompalla protested.

"He is truly a count whereas I am only the son of one. I like to tease him about it." I winked slyly to my brother bishop and patted him on the shoulder. Rompalla wiped his hand over his face, but I saw he was smiling.

"In any case, His Eminence is here because as Secretary of State he must be present to witness the personal gift We wish to give you."

"And what gift might that be?" Holmes' gaze fixed on the square black velvet-covered box that Rampalla took from the desk behind him, and his eyes narrowed a trifle. "Surely that could not be what its appearance suggests. It looks quite…official, I fear."

"And would that be cause for alarm, Signore?"

"I beg your pardon, Holiness. I do not mean to insult your evident generosity. But I have little interest in official honours arising from my profession. If it were otherwise, I would have long ago ceased to assist Scotland Yard." He smiled.

"What We propose to present you, Signore, is, I admit, an official honour. But it comes from a personal sense of gratitude for your assistance. It has a ribbon attached to it, but no strings. It requires no gesture of fealty on your part to Us or Our faith. What We give is a gift from Our heart to yours, in appreciation, and in recognition of a quality We saw in you from the moment you entered Our presence—your nobility."

I took the box from Rompalla and stepped closer to Holmes. "You referred to chess, so I will admit that this quest for an English cathedral started when We sent a bishop as envoy to Victoria on the occasion of her jubilee. Then, like a pawn, We sent out a courier with the cameos, only to have them stolen away by a thieving rook. Our next play is to send a *knight*." I opened the case revealing an eight-pointed blue enamelled star, touched with 18 karat gold flames in between the star's rays. The centre of the star, adorned in white mother of pearl read in gold "Pius IX" with the words "*Virtuiti et Merito*" encircling it. The thick ribbon of the decoration was dark blue silk bordered with red.

"While this is given to Catholics, it is the highest honour We can also bestow on someone who is not Catholic. The Knightly Order of Pius was formed by Pius V, and Our predecessor Pius IX had it reconstituted. It is intended to bless those who have done a great personal service to the pope, the papacy, and the children of God. You have done all of these, my son, and you most certainly deserve it.

"However, We do fear negative consequences for you if news of a papal knighthood is revealed. The British Government may not see it in a favourable light. For that reason We would have you be '*cavaliere in pectore*,' a knight of Our heart— one in secret. Only Rompalla and I will know, and though your name will be recorded in the order, it will never be revealed to anyone else unless We know you approve."

Holmes still appeared reticent. "I—"

"Please do not refuse, Signore. You would break my heart. It is all I can think of to honour you to my satisfaction."

He sighed. "Then, I will accept, Your Holiness."

"*Grazie*, my son. For this we will need your full Christian name."

"William Sherlock Scott Holmes."

As Rompalla scribbled it down on a piece of paper, I mused, "So many consonants—how does one say all of them?"

"It is much easier to say than Gioacchino Vincenzo Raffaele Luigi Pecci," Holmes replied, taking care to pronounce every syllable of my given name with dramatic flair.

"Ha! Touché. That's one of the reasons We chose the short name of Leo for Our pontificate." When His Eminence finished writing, I handed the box back to him, opened it, and lifted out the decoration. "Won't you please kneel, my son?"

Holmes raised an eyebrow.

"We ask you only so We might bestow a proper apostolic blessing upon you. That is all."

He did kneel, looking exceedingly uncomfortable as I stepped in front of him. I laid the ribbon and medal around his collar and said, "We, Leo XIII, from the chair of Peter, do bestow upon you, William Sherlock Scott Holmes, the title of Knight of the Order of Pius IX, and render upon you Our apostolic blessing." I touched my right hand upon his head. "May the Lord bless you and keep you, may he make his face shine upon you and be gracious to you, may he look upon you with kindness and grant you his peace, and may Almighty God bless you." I made the sign of the cross. "*In nomine Patris, et Filii, et Spiritus Sancti. Amen.* You may stand now, Sir Sherlock Holmes of the Ordo Pianus."

He stood and said in a hoarse voice, "Thank you, Your Holiness"

I winked. "You may want to remove that trinket before you board the train. It may draw some attention."

Holmes removed the decoration and placed it in its box, which he then slipped into his right jacket pocket.

"One more thing, Signore." I placed my hand on his shoulder. "As you are *in pectore*, there is a promise to you. Should you need any assistance at all, if you are in trouble and you need help, if you require anything, you need only send Us a wire or letter signing it as *cavalieri in pectore*, and We will do all We can to aid you. This promise is from Us and any who succeed Us."

"Thank you, Holiness. I will remember that."

I then gave him the cameo case. "Now go to Her Majesty with Our heartfelt good wishes, and be well. We will be sending a telegram to Cardinal Manning to expect you so he might join you when you visit her. I hope I may see you again, my son."

"And I, you, Holy Father."

Knowing the English do not prefer the continental form of saying goodbye by kissing both cheeks, I gripped his hand warmly, and he left my presence. I found it remarkable how in such a short period of time I'd become so fond of him, but then, his genius had inspired me. Despite his scientific, intellectual aloofness, his heart was all too clear. Especially now that I made a startling realisation.

He'd called me Holy Father.

I smiled, a new joy illuminating my heart. For I felt there was great hope for England, if such people were born of her.

Rendered complete into Our memoir on the 10th day of July in the year 1888, the eleventh of our pontificate.

: *Leo P. P. XIII* :

FINALE

Sherlock Holmes set Leo's memoir on the table next to his armchair and looked over at Deacon Brown and myself. He'd returned in the midst of our tea and I'd eagerly shared with him His Holiness's story.

"Well?" I asked.

"Well what, Watson?"

"Is it true?"

He frowned. "Do you think His Holiness is a liar? Of course it's true."

"You have a papal knighthood and you didn't tell me?"

Holmes stood and walked briskly across the room to the Persian slipper of tobacco hanging at the fireplace, where he filled his clay pipe. "It was something personal between His Holiness and me," he said. "He gave it to me to honour me and I received it out of respect for him. It has little value other than that."

"Surely not," I protested.

"*That's* why I didn't tell you." Seeing my wounded expression he added, "Of course I am glad that you now know. His Holiness knows I trust you, and he's right. I should have shared it with you a long time ago. I simply didn't want you to make of it more than it is to me." He turned his gaze to Deacon Brown. "But I am sure he didn't anticipate you reading his tale as well. You realise you must say nothing of this to anyone."

"Since you are *in pectore*, Mr. Holmes, I could only reveal this story on pain of excommunication."

"Well, that is incentive to remain silent, I would say."

"You said you received it out of respect for him," Brown said. "Is that to mean there are those from whom you'd refuse such an honour?"

"Without question." Holmes frowned. "But this man—" He pointed to the photo of Leo on the mantelpiece. "This man is different. Noble and kingly, yes—he is nobility after all. But he has a very keen mind coupled with a truly pious soul. He was legitimate in all he said and did, and I could not help but respect him. I even said as much to Her Majesty when Cardinal Manning and I brought the cameos to her."

I straightened in my chair. "Really? What happened?"

"Well, she was very impressed with the cameos. Since it is her favourite jewellery, she was awed by them, I think, and moved that he'd choose something that she loved so much personally as a gift to her people. So she asked me my impression of His Holiness. I told her that the man personally faced down a notorious killer to save a man in mortal danger over those cameos, and that he was a genuinely good man. I also said that if he asked her anything in the future she should keep in mind that he is the sort who will only speak and act out of love and nothing more."

"You fought for his cause," Brown said. "You took a chance, Mr. Holmes."

"I did, and the Prime Minister was fit to be tied. My brother was uncomfortable about it as well, but I told him that I could only be truthful about the situation."

"Mycroft doesn't know about the knighthood?"

Holmes shook his head. "It's probably best he doesn't know considering those with whom he deals on a regular basis."

"And now the cornerstone has been laid here in Westminster," Brown said.

"Yes." Holmes smiled.

"Thank you, Mr. Holmes," Deacon Brown said. His eyelids fluttered behind his spectacles. He seemed moved. "Thank you so very much."

"You're welcome, of course."

"Pardon me, Holmes," I said. "But—may we see it?"

"See it?"

"The decoration you received for you knighthood."

"If you must." Holmes went to his desk and pulled out the drawer containing many mementos from his cases. From the very back of the drawer he removed a now dusty, black velvet box. He placed it in my hands and Brown and I both marvelled at the lovely ornament contained within.

"It has come in handy," Holmes remarked. "The actual knighthood, that is, not the trinket."

"Really?"

"When I went into hiding after the death of Moriarty, you'll remember I went first to Florence. From there I sent a wire to Mycroft, but I also sent one to Cardinal Rompalla thinking aid from the Vatican may reach me more quickly. Rompalla was a better choice, as sending it to the Pope directly might raise eyebrows at the hotel. I signed the telegram as His Holiness advised. It has never been revealed, of course, Watson, that the Norwegian explorer Sigerson conducted his travels with Vatican identity papers."

"You're not serious."

"Oh, I am. The morning after I sent my wire to the Vatican, a courier showed up at my hotel with a packet of items I found invaluable. Money, of course—several hundred thousand lire—identification with the name I'd indicated to him, and a letter of introduction from the Pope himself that guaranteed me entry to any church institution in Christendom. I did my share of staying in monasteries, and found it a rather peaceful experience every time. Also in the packet was a medal of Saint Michael, which I think the Holy Father threw in for good measure. I put that on my watch chain with Mrs. Norton's sovereign." He grinned. "In any event, I travelled all around the world with Vatican papers as identification. No one was the wiser. But I will admit this to you—" He paused and continued wistfully, "I spent two full years in Tibet, Watson. Met with the head Lama, if you'll recall. I also went to Mecca. But in all that time, while it all was greatly enlightening and rewarding for me, I would say that I never truly experienced such profound holiness as I did in one day in this man's presence." He tapped the photograph with the stem of his pipe. "I keep his photograph here to remind me that people like him really do walk the Earth. It gives me hope."

"I'd have to agree, Holmes. After meeting him myself, I felt the same way. That's why I asked for this story. But it seems it'll be going into my old dispatch box at Charing Cross with all the other tales of a sensitive nature."

"That box is probably pretty cramped by now," Holmes mused.

"Yes, well. I've been thinking I should procure a larger one."

"I think that would be wise, old friend," Holmes said, lighting his pipe with an amused glimmer in his eyes. "Immeasurably wise."

The Second
Coptic Patriarch

"You know that I am preoccupied with this case of the two Coptic Patriarchs, which should come to a head to-day."

— Sherlock Holmes,
"The Retired Colourman"

IT WAS A WARM JULY DAY in 1898 when the bell rang downstairs waking me from a heat-induced afternoon slumber on our sitting room couch. No clients had graced Holmes' consulting room for the week preceding save for a seven-year-old boy who'd come to ask Holmes' assistance in finding his lost kitten (a problem Holmes graciously solved for the tearful lad without leaving our lodgings). I was hopeful the stall in business had reached its end.

Holmes made a languid stretch and straightened in his chair. "I do hope the bell means a problem of interest, Watson. There is little of significance in the morning papers." He tossed aside the early edition of the *Times* that he'd spread across his knees.

Our page brought in a card.

"Hm. M. Duroc. No occupation. Show him in, Billy."

The boy opened the door for a swarthy man of about thirty years in age wearing a finely-tailored grey suit. His thick, bland face, which sported a Bohemian-style beard, was clouded with a troubled expression. His most striking feature was his impressive height, which I surmised was above six feet. Under his arm was a folded newspaper and he carried a heavy walking stick in his right hand, the knob of which was studded with a blue jewel.

"Thank you for seeing me, gentlemen." The man spoke in a

velvety, deep voice, thick with a Gallic accent. "I hope I have not interrupted anything."

"Not at all, Monsieur," I said. "We are grateful for the company. Won't you please sit down?"

As the gentleman took a seat near the fireplace, Holmes rose from his chair and walked across the room to his desk. When he turned again to face us, he was aiming his revolver at our guest.

"Holmes!" I cried.

"Block the door, Watson. No, Monsieur, stay right where you are. Did you think I'd not recognize your voice the moment you spoke? You may have been in disguise when I last encountered you, but your height and voice are unmistakable."

I gazed in alarm at our visitor who remained, as Holmes ordered, quite still in his chair.

"Who is he?" I asked.

"Does the name *Flambeau* strike a cord, Watson?"

"Not the notorious—" I began.

"Thief," our guest finished for me. "I am. Though I retired from that profession six months ago."

"Retired?" Holmes snorted. "I suppose you could retire quite comfortably considering the countless treasures you've stolen. You are one of the slipperiest there has ever been. That you eluded me when I last encountered you is evidence of that. Your only saving grace is that you are not a killer. You do realize I could hand you over to the Yard right now for walking in that door?"

Flambeau nodded. "I knew there was a strong possibility you'd deduce who I was—"

"Indeed."

"Mr. Holmes, whatever justice done to me is well-deserved. But there is a man who sits in prison right now who, unlike me, does not deserve to be there. I came because I know you are the one man who could free him."

"You took a considerable risk."

"He would have taken it for me; I can do no less. Besides, from what I have read in the good doctor's narratives, you are a man of honour and justice. I believed the risk was worth it."

After eyeing our visitor an additional moment, Holmes returned to his chair and placed the gun near his hand on the table next to him. "I assume Duroc is your real name?"

"Yes." Flambeau's posture was rigid, the only sign that he was perhaps a bit more nervous than he first appeared. "Have you read the afternoon edition of the *Times?*" he asked.

"Our page has not yet brought it up."

"Then allow me." He handed Holmes the paper he'd held under his arm. "This article here is the one of interest." He pointed to the thin right column on the front page.

"'Egyptian Clerk Murdered in Paddington.'" Holmes read the article. "How does this concern you?"

"Actually it concerns my friend. He has been arrested for the murder. You can read it all in the article. And while you might think I would only have criminal friends considering my former occupation, I would assure you the gentleman in question is not. He is, in fact, a good and noble Catholic priest who has become a bit of a detective in his own right. I believe you know him. Reverend Father J. Paul Brown?"

"Father Brown?" I repeated. "Is he a podgy young gentleman with glasses and an innocent face?"

"That would be he."

Holmes grunted. "Dr. Watson and I have met him a few years ago briefly prior to his ordination. At the time he expressed an enthusiasm for my work, but I did not know he intended to pursue the same study."

"To be honest, I do not believe the good reverend father intended to pursue it at all, though he has always been an enthusiast of the topic. Cardinal Vaughn discovered his gift for unravelling little mysteries while he was still in seminary and decided that he would serve the Church best as a 'problem solver,' if you will. His Eminence dispatches him to clarify situations and make sense of them. He often places him in troubled parishes to set them right, though situations of a criminal nature often fall in his lap as well; thefts, murders, and such. That is how he caught me, in fact—by happenstance. I had nearly walked out of an exclusive club with a priceless collection of rare silver, but he confronted me and made me realize...." Flambeau hesitated, then continued in a quiet voice. "Sir, he told me everything I'd ever done and why. He understood. That is why I had to come today."

Holmes's eyes narrowed. "He understood? What do you mean?"

"He has a certain...empathy...with those who commit the darkest of sins. I know he would not commit them, and yet he would tell you that he could. That, I fear, is the trouble here."

Holmes and I looked at each other, then back to the thief.

"Pray, go on, Monsieur."

"Father Brown and I knew the victim, Mr. Sharif Fouad. He was a clerk at a book shop that specializes in rare volumes. Brown often patronized the establishment, though to my memory he purchased only a few books there. I went to the shop with him a few times myself and usually, after looking at a couple volumes of interest, he'd spend his time speaking to Fouad, the proprietor Mr. Rareburton, or Rareburton's son Charles. Rareburton is a well-educated fellow, a staunch Anglican, and he and his son both have a great interest in church matters. They liked to have friendly debates with Brown. And Fouad liked to provide his Coptic Orthodox thoughts in the argument. Apparently he'd spent time in a Coptic monastery. It made for some lively conversation. As I recall Mr. Rareburton's dear wife often pleaded for the discussions to end, for they would go long after business hours infringing on her planned supper time.

"In any event, Fouad wrote Father Brown one day last week. I was with him when Fouad's note arrived and he shared it with me. Fouad had heard news that His Holiness Pope Leo XIII had approved a Coptic bishop, a convert from the Coptic Orthodox Church, to take the Patriarchate of Coptic Catholics in Cairo under the name Cyril II to rival the Patriarch of the Coptic Orthodox Church who took the name Cyril V.

"This new Coptic patriarch is a man Fouad knew from his youth, apparently. In his letter, Fouad wrote that there was something scandalous about this Cyril II, something he wanted to share with Father Brown in private. He said he hoped Brown could inform Cardinal Vaughn, and he likewise, the Pope—" Flambeau smirked at the thought. "The poor fellow did not realize how far-fetched the idea was, but Brown did not seem daunted. In any case, Brown made an appointment with the Egyptian to meet at the book shop before it opened. Fouad asked Brown to come alone and not tell the proprietor or his son about the meeting. When Father Brown arrived there, he found Fouad dead; a clean strike to the temple had killed him instantly."

"Inconvenient."

"Very. In any case, when I saw the afternoon paper I rushed to Scotland Yard. I was allowed to meet with him in his cell. When I asked him what happened, he said only that he went to meet the man and found him dead. He would say no more."

"You walked into Scotland Yard?" I asked.

Flambeau glanced over at me with a sly smile. "Of course. They have no idea what I look like."

Holmes released a sardonic chuckle. "You are a man of nerve."

"I should have some nerve to do what I have done, no?"

"No doubt. Is there more to this story?"

Flambeau's dark eyebrows furrowed. "Brown was not the one who telephoned the Yard about the murder. Someone else did, and the Yard doesn't know who. Only Brown was present when they arrived and he refused to speak to them about the incident. He'd only say he'd come to meet the victim at his request and found him as he was.

"But I know Father Brown. I know he saw something else. Unfortunately he had on his person the letter from the victim asking to meet him, and you know how Inspector Lestrade does his work—"

Holmes looked away and sighed.

"They arrested Brown on the spot, and as Father will say nothing of what he found on the matter, his case looks grim."

"Did Lestrade put forth a motive?"

Flambeau shook his head. "He said he'd find out what it was eventually, though he hinted that Fouad probably knew something scandalous about Brown's personal life. Of course I know any such theory is entirely without basis."

"And you are certain Brown found something that would lead to the killer."

"With Brown there is no way he could not. He is like you in that regard. He observes even when he does not mean to."

"Nevertheless, he told you nothing more."

"Correct."

Holmes sat silently for a moment, his brow wrinkled in thought. Suddenly he jumped to his feet and stuffed the gun into his coat pocket. "Let's visit that book shop. After that we shall go to Scotland Yard. Bring your notebook, Watson."

We made our way in a growler to a shop known as Curious Books on Harrow Road in Paddington. Scotland Yard had already left, but the shop was being watched by a constable until the proprietor returned from his questioning. After a quick discussion with the constable, we were allowed to enter the small, brown brick building. Holmes *tsk*ed, disapprovingly at the scene that met his eyes.

"As I suspected, a herd of Spanish bulls could have done less damage to this place," he said. "Nevertheless, I can see that there was a struggle. Look how the book case is pushed out of position—and scuff marks on the floor there." He looked around at the markings on the floor around a puddle of blood where the victim's body had lain. He paced around the mess almost on tip-toe, then stopped and crouched.

"What sort of boots does the reverend father wear, Flambeau?"

"He has small feet," the Frenchman replied. "Usually short boots with round toes."

"Then this is where he crouched as he inspected the body," Holmes said, indicating two smudged footprints tinged with blood. "He stepped in the blood by accident as he entered the room. It was probably dark in here at the time. There is another toe smudge here from what appears to be a long, thin foot, pointed toe boot—rather slender. They seemed to have stepped out from the area of the bookcase. Too bad it isn't a complete footprint. And there are scuff marks from the heels of another boot here."

Holmes straightened, and walking once more around the puddle of gore on the tile, he examined the book case just beyond it.

"Interesting. There is a book missing."

"How can you tell, Holmes? The books are all knocked about—as you say, the bookcase shifted."

He pointed to a large gap among the volumes. "Yes, but this gap here, Watson—many of the books toppled over into it. Let me see if I am correct."

He walked along the bookcase and turned behind the shop counter where he bent over to rummage through items out of my view.

"Ah! Excellent. As I suspected." He rose and dropped an exceedingly large dusty tome onto the counter.

"What is that, Holmes?"

"The murder weapon."

"What?" Flambeau examined the book. "I see...there is blood here on the corner of the binding. But why did Scotland Yard not find it?"

"Because they did not look. They did not bother. The newspaper said Lestrade believed Brown had used his umbrella to strike the victim. But whoever used this knew it was too valuable to throw away even if it was to cover his tracks. He tried to wipe it off, as you see, but did not finish. He put it hastily under the counter when our Father Brown surprised him with his arrival."

"You think Brown saw the killer?" I asked.

"Anything is possible, Watson." Holmes chuckled and flipped open the book. "*The Rule of Oliver Cromwell*—weighty subject, no doubt."

"What do you want in here?"

All three of us looked to the door. A gentleman of about five and fifty, dressed in charcoal tweed, had entered the shop with an attractive, ebony-haired woman of middle years on his arm. Despite her almost exotic colouring, she seemed pale. She fingered what looked like a silver religious medal around her neck as she gazed at us with black eyes that were red-rimmed from tears. It seemed to me she was still shocked at the horror committed in their establishment.

Meanwhile, a younger, slender man of twenty, who bore a strong resemblance to the elder, stood at his other elbow. The young man's dark eyes locked upon the book on the counter.

"The Cromwell book…" he muttered.

"Good afternoon," said Holmes. "Allow me introduce myself. I am Sherlock Holmes. This my associate, Dr. Watson, and I believe you know Monsieur Duroc."

"I do." Rareburton shot a cool glare at Flambeau and returned his gaze to Holmes. "As you are not Scotland Yard, you have no business here."

"In fact, I do. I have been asked to look into this case."

"By whom? Scotland Yard has already made its arrest."

"I am here on behalf of the accused. Monsieur Duroc has engaged me."

Rareburton snorted. "I thought as much. In that case I would ask you to kindly leave the premises."

"Gerald, really," said his wife in a trembling voice. I noticed that she spoke with a sleight foreign accent, the origin of which was familiar to me though I could not recall exactly where I'd heard the like before. "Must you be so rude?"

"Never fear, Madame, we were just leaving," Holmes said. Tucking the book under his elbow, he started to the door. But Rareburton grabbed his arm.

"Where are you going with that book? It is an expensive volume."

"It was used to murder your associate. I am taking it to Scotland Yard."

Rareburton did not seem phased by this revelation. "And who will reimburse me for it?"

"You will have to take that up with Inspector Lestrade, I suppose. Though I assume you will have to mark it as a loss in your ledger, because most likely it will not be returned." Holmes' eyes turned to the youth. "This must be your son, Charles."

Rareburton scowled. "Yes."

"How do you do, young man?" said Holmes. "You have quite a bruise there on your neck. How did you manage that?"

The young man touched the area on his throat. "Playing cricket with some of my mates, sir. Bowler went a little wild."

"That would smart, I would say. Are you at university then?"

"I am at Camford on scholarship, where I study theology," he said. "At this moment I am on holiday."

"Indeed? And this Cromwell book was of interest to you?"

Charles shook his head. "I've looked at it from time to time. I simply noticed it missing when we came here after the incident."

"One would think," Rareburton interrupted, "that if you were so practiced at deducing the truth of people, Mr. Holmes, you'd already know what you need to know about my son without asking so many questions."

Holmes smiled. "Indeed, I have already deduced much, Mr. Rareburton. About him, your wife, and you."

"Oh?" Rareburton crossed his arms. "For instance?"

"For instance you were once an officer in Her Majesty's Army. You served in Egypt in the forces under Gordon, but you were not there more than a year or two. You left the Army at the same level at which you entered it. You were an educated man, however, and in an attempt to recover from you disappointing exit from the military you decided to make a living for yourself as a dealer of rare books. Shall I go on?"

"Who have you been speaking to?" Rareburton snarled. "You've been snooping into my past."

"Hardly. I observed it all from your appearance. Your bearing is that of a military man and you carry a handkerchief in your sleeve—two characteristics my old friend Dr. Watson shares with you. You are an educated gentleman, therefore an officer. That you are now the proprietor of a book shop and not in a higher situation in life informs me of a discharge from the military that did not set you on a brighter path. And your turn in Egypt is evident form the unique tattoo of an Egyptian hieroglyph on the underside of your right wrist."

Rareburton's face suddenly flushed red with rage. He thrust his index finger into Holmes face. "Get out."

"As I said, we were about to go," Holmes said with a grin. "Gentlemen, shall we?" He led us out the door to the street.

"He was rather warm," I remarked.

Holmes chuckled. "Indeed, Watson. All of it is interesting, of course."

"Do you make anything of it yet, Mr. Holmes?" asked Flambeau.

"Not yet, not yet. I need more data." He hailed a four-wheeler to take us to Scotland Yard.

After waiting half an hour we obtained an order to visit the imprisoned priest and Lestrade himself escorted the three of us to the man's cell.

"He has been as quiet as a church mouse," Lestrade said, amused at his own attempt at humour. "I ask him questions and he simply blinks at me. Bloody frustrating." With a jangle of keys, he unlocked the cell.

"Thank you, Lestrade," Holmes said. "May we speak to him alone?"

Lestrade shrugged. "If you wish." He waved us inside and closed the door with a hard clang behind us.

Brown sat in the corner of his cell beneath a gas lamp, quietly reading his breviary. He stood when we entered. "Mr. Holmes, Dr. Watson, what a pleasant surprise. How are you? Monsieur Duroc, you did not summon these gentlemen on my account did you?"

"I had to do something, Father," said Flambeau.

Brown sighed and shook his head.

"Father Brown," said Holmes. "Your friend took a great risk coming to me. He apparently puts great value in his friendship with you."

"Yes, yes. I know he does."

"Then you must not despair—" I said.

"Despair?" Brown's grey eyes blinked at me from behind his spectacles. "I do not despair, Doctor. I am precisely where I ought to be."

"Allow us to be the judge of that," said Holmes. "I would like to ask you a few questions, if I may."

"I will answer what I can, Mr. Holmes."

"Excellent. As I understand it, Mr. Fouad wrote you and asked you to meet him early this morning before the book shop opened."

"That is correct."

"And when you arrived, you found him already dead."

"Yes."

"According to the newspaper account, he was struck in the temple, is that so?"

"I fear so."

"Such a blow with a pointed heavy object would kill him instantly. I found the murder weapon."

"Oh, did you?"

Holmes held it up. "Yes. It was hidden under the counter. I take it you searched for it?"

"Things progressed rather quickly—"

"As I suspected. Did you observe anything at the crime scene that might be of use to me?" Holmes' eyes gleamed with an intense twinkle. "You do know what I mean, do you not?"

"I do, Mr. Holmes" Brown replied. "I saw nothing I can mention."

"But surely you saw *something*. Your friend believes you did." Holmes voice dropped. "Or perhaps you saw…*someone?*"

Brown's youthful, round face went utterly vacant of expression. He blinked at my friend from behind his spectacles and said nothing.

Holmes' eyes narrowed. "You saw the murderer, didn't you?"

The priest still said nothing. He did not twitch. Standing stock still, his face was as blank as a sheet of clean paper.

Holmes nodded. "Thank you. The situation is quite clear to me now."

Brown's shoulders drooped and his eyebrows furrowed.

"No, no, none of that, Father," Holmes said. "You cannot help what I deduce on my own, and if necessary I shall testify to that effect to your superiors. Right now I shall follow this from my end." He went to the door, where he turned back to the cleric. "I'll have you out of here soon. Be assured of it."

BROWN'S SHOULDERS DROOPED AND HIS EYEBROWS FURROWED.

In the hall, I asked, "Holmes, I do not understand what that last bit was about."

"Nor do I," said Flambeau.

"It is not mine to reveal. Father Brown keeps it to himself and so shall I until matters become clear."

He led the way to Lestrade's office, and the official detective looked up at us with a grin as we entered. "So, did our church mouse say anything to you?"

"I did not expect him to, Lestrade. May we see the victim's body?"

"You are taking his case?"

"Of course. He is an innocent man."

Lestrade chuckled. "Mr. Holmes, you are welcome to look. The Egyptian's body is in the morgue. You know the way. Of course, I do not see how you can prove this man's innocence. We have the letter inviting Brown to the scene of the crime at the time the murder was committed. We have his umbrella with a heavy hooked handle that could have brained the fellow—"

"No, Fouad was struck with this." Holmes dropped the enormous book on the desk. Lestrade started at the thud it made. "It was hidden behind the shop counter. Please note the blood on the binding." Leaving Lestrade slack-jawed and staring at the book, Holmes turned out the door and headed down the hall to the morgue.

The coroner who knew my friend and me allowed the three of us to enter the small inner examination room where the body had been stored. Holmes pulled back the white sheet covering the body to reveal a rather slight gentleman with black, curly hair and light almandine skin. His temple, as the paper reported, was indeed crushed in on the left side.

Holmes glanced at that, then pointed to the man's cheeks. "Notice the scratches, gentlemen."

"Those are fresh," I said. "Someone clawed his face during the scuffle."

"So it would seem. Hello, what's this?" He had now moved to the man's arm, and was holding up his right wrist. On the underside of it was a tattoo in the pattern of what appeared to be a simple hieroglyph:

"Interesting," he said. "Mr. Rareburton had the very same tattoo on the inner portion of his right wrist." Holmes took a small notebook from his pocket and sketched the symbol with a stub pencil. He then stuffed the notebook in his pocket and dusted his hands. "Gentleman, I must go my own way for a couple of hours. Would the two of you mind so much doing something together to expedite this case?"

I glanced at Flambeau and he to me. He gave a quick nod.

"What would you have us do, Holmes?" I asked.

Holmes leaned on the table, paying no mind to the corpse beside him. "I want you to return to the book shop and convince Mr. Rareburton to accompany you to Baker Street for an interview."

"Considering how inhospitable the fellow was, I doubt he'll agree to that."

My friend clapped me on the shoulder. "I have faith in you, Watson. After so many years with me I have no doubt you'll succeed. Besides, you are a man of words yourself and you have the clever Monsieur Duroc to assist you."

I sighed. "Very well, Holmes. I shall come up with something."

"Good man. Let us be on our way, then. I shall see you in Baker Street."

As Holmes requested, Flambeau and I returned to the book shop. When we entered the establishment, the senior Rareburton was standing on a stool wearing a shopkeeper's apron organizing the books on the higher shelves that had been tossed about in the early-morning conflict. Already the puddle of blood had been mopped from the floor and the books on the lower shelves straightened.

"Back again?" Rareburton glared at the two of us and stepped down from the stool. "Where is your observant friend?"

"He had some other business to attend to, Mr. Rareburton, but he asked if you would be so kind as to accompany us so he might ask you a few questions about the case."

He crossed his arms. "I thought he'd already deduced everything from meeting me the first time."

At this moment Mrs. Rareburton stepped out from behind the book cases, followed by her son. The woman held more books in her arms, and her body trembled as if with cold.

"What questions does he have?" his wife asked. Her voice

quaked and her dark eyes sparkled with concern. "Surely anything he needs to know can be found at Scotland Yard."

Flambeau chuckled beside me. "Mr. Holmes and the Yard rarely come to the same conclusions, Madame."

"Sherlock Holmes is requesting this interview because he wants to accuse my father," young Charles Rareburton said.

"Not necessarily, young man," I said. "Sometimes Mr. Holmes interviews those around the situation to get the information he needs to find the culprit. There is a possibility your father knows something and does not realise it. That has happened in more cases than I can count."

"Besides," added Flambeau, "Your father was a good friend of Mr. Fouad."

"I was," Mr. Rareburton said. "He was almost a brother to me."

"What motive would you have to kill him?"

"None."

"Then surely you have nothing to fear from an interview with Mr. Holmes."

Rareburton sighed.

"Mr. Rareburton," Flambeau pressed. "I know you want to see the man who truly committed the crime punished. If my friend is innocent, does he deserve to hang for something he did not do, while the man who killed your friend runs free?"

Rareburton considered this a moment. He removed his dusty apron and placed it on the counter. "Very well."

His wife placed her books on the counter and followed Rareburton as he walked across the shop to the coat rack. "Gerald," she protested in a weak voice. "You are not really going to go, are you?"

"If it means they will leave us alone from now on, then it is well worth it. I have nothing to fear from this amateur detective."

He snatched up his jacket and hat. As he did this, I glanced at his wrist. Holmes was right—of course. The tattoo was there, barely visible just below his shirt cuff.

We took our waiting four-wheeler, and when we arrived at Baker Street, I asked Mrs. Hudson to provide us with tea while we waited for my friend to arrive. During our repast, Rareburton remained mostly silent, his sharp blue eyes gazing around at the objects of interest on the wall and shelves as he sipped his beverage.

Finally he asked, "Who are all these people?" He gestured around at the collection of portraits adorning our walls.

"Other than General Gordon with whom you are familiar and Reverend Henry Ward Beecher over there upon my shelf, the rest are various notorious criminals."

Rareburton grunted. "You find them all of interest, I suppose?"

"Me? Not entirely. Those are Holmes' pictures. General Gordon and Reverend Beecher are mine."

"I see." He returned his gaze to me. "You were a military man, or so your friend implied."

"I served as an army surgeon in Afghanistan."

"Really? Where?"

"Maiwand."

Rareburton's eyes widened with surprise. "You are lucky to be sitting here."

"I have often said so."

He sighed and rested back in his chair in thoughtful silence for a short moment. Then he said, "Your friend was right, you know. I was discharged from my commission—for reasons of which I am not proud. In fact, if things had not changed, there is every possibility I may have someday ended up as one of these portraits here."

"We have all done things we regret," Flambeau said in a quiet voice. I glanced over at the thief. His eyes were downcast.

"Indeed," I said.

The door to the sitting room then opened and Holmes entered followed by Inspector Lestrade and a manacled Father Brown.

"Excellent work, gentlemen." Holmes smiled. "Mr. Rareburton, so good to see you again."

Rareburton did not return the jovial greeting. "What is Brown doing here?"

"Mr. Holmes convinced me to bring him along." Lestrade grumbled. "Wanted him to be present for another one of his startling revelations, I suppose."

Holmes chuckled. "Ah, now, Lestrade, you are an honest man. Tell me truthfully, do you not want justice to prevail? I know you do."

"Then let's get on with it," Lestrade said in a weary tone. The Yard detective guided Father Brown to a chair in the corner, and the priest sat quietly, resting his handcuffed wrists in his lap.

"Certainly. Let me begin by saying that I am grateful, Mr. Rareburton, that you came. Your presence will bring forth the guilty party in this case."

"I should hope so. While you may not consider me well-placed in society as a shop-keeper, my time is of value to me."

"No doubt, no doubt," Holmes agreed amiably. "Let me therefore request that you tell us about the Brotherhood of *Sa*."

Rareburton went rigid. His jaw clamped shut tight.

"As I suspected," Holmes said, "you will say nothing. You are bound by an oath to remain silent on it. I, of course, have taken no such oath, so I will be happy to explain who the Brotherhood are to the rest of my guests." He produced the notebook drawing that he'd made of the hieroglyph and held it up to everyone. "This Egyptian hieroglyph is *Sa*," Holmes explained. "It means 'protection.' It is not in and of itself an evil marking, quite the opposite really. But it would seem a secret society known as the The Brotherhood of *Sa* has taken it for its identifying mark. The members of their group tattoo this hieroglyph on the inner portion of their right wrists. Both Mr. Rareburton and his friend Mr. Fouad have this very tattoo.

"The Brotherhood is a gang, a bit of an Egyptian 'mafia' one might say, that bullies protection money out of business owners in Cairo and Alexandria. Loosely modelled on the Masons, they take oaths and such. I learned about them as I did my research on the symbol at the British Museum only an hour ago. When our military came to occupy Alexandria and Cairo, the Brotherhood recruited British soldiers to aid them in terrorizing locals for money. As the Brotherhood had grown quite wealthy in its endeavours, avarice lured a small number British soldiers to their cause, enough to make the Brotherhood's threats even more effective."

Holmes turned to his guest. "When your participation in these activities was discovered, Mr. Rareburton, you were told that your services in Her Majesty's Army were no longer required. Is that not so?"

"I fail to see what this has to do with Mr. Fouad's death," Rareburton replied.

"You met Fouad when you were in Egypt."

"That goes without saying."

"Why did he come to England?"

"A better life, or so he said. He did not want to serve the Brotherhood anymore. They only operate in Egypt and he thought England was as good a choice as any to start a new life. He knew several soldiers from the Brotherhood—"

"And yet he sought you out."

"He was what I would call a friend, and he knew I had no love for the gang as it had nearly destroyed me."

"No doubt. But there was more to this friendship, was there not?"

Suddenly the door burst open and Charles Rareburton stumbled into the room, panting.

"Charles!" Rareburton rose from his chair. "What the devil are you doing here?"

Charles lifted his right hand, bringing it into view. He was holding a revolver. "Let my father go," he said, pointing the weapon at Holmes. "He's innocent."

"First of all, young man," Holmes snapped impatiently. "No one is holding your father here against his will. Secondly, I already know he's innocent."

"He is?" Lestrade, Flambeau, and I said together.

"Then why the deuce did you bring him here?" Lestrade went on. "Why did you insist we come here? What sort of game is this, Holmes?"

"It is no game, Lestrade," Holmes replied. "Mr. Rareburton's past is important to this case. Nevertheless, I am biding my time while we await the appearance of the actual killer."

All eyes in the room went to young Charles, who glanced down at the gun he held in his own hand. He blanched and lowered the weapon.

"Charles," Rareburton whispered.

"No, no," said Holmes. "It is not he."

"It isn't?" Several voices asked at once.

"No. Though I have a theory as to why Mr. Fouad attacked the young man and nearly strangled the life out of him." Holmes crossed his arms. "Cricket incident indeed."

"Strangled him?" Rareburton repeated. "He attacked you, Charles?" he asked his son.

"The marks on his neck, of course," Holmes said. "And the dried blood in his fingernails from the scratches he made on Mr. Fouad's face. Charles has washed his hands several times since the incident, but there still are traces there if you will observe."

"Why the devil did he attack you?" Rareburton asked.

"He—I—" Charles eyes turned desperately from his father to the quiet priest sitting in the corner. The priest only retuned his gaze with blinking eyes.

"I can't say," Charles whispered.

Holmes sighed and shook his head.

"Listen, boy," said Lestrade as he rose from his seat and approached the lad. "If it was an act of self defence, you are not at fault. You might as well reveal all."

"This isn't about me," Charles returned quickly.

"No? Then who is it about?" Lestrade said, his voice rising in pitch.

Charles looked at the floor. "I c-cannot say."

"Why the devil not?" Lestrade demanded. "Young man, you just burst in here waving a gun about. I have every reason to drag you down to Scotland Yard right now. If you had something to do with this whole mess, why do you not speak up?"

"It is a circle of silence, Lestrade," Holmes said.

"I am not such a complete dullard that I cannot see that, Holmes," Lestrade returned. "But why?"

"Such pacts are made to protect someone. In this case, it was made to protect a man who made, himself, an oath. And it is because of that oath that they must remain silent."

"You're speaking of me," said Rareburton.

"Of course," Holmes said. "You have taken an oath of silence as we know. And, I would presume that you took an oath of vengeance as well."

"Oath of vengeance?" Flambeau finally spoke. "Do you mean the sort of oath that if one of their members are injured or killed they must enact revenge on whoever committed the assault?"

"Precisely," said Holmes. "These sorts of things are common. Even the Masons have something of that ilk in their rituals. And our little silent circle here wants to prevent Mr. Rareburton from heeding his oath, for he is a man of his word. If he knows who killed Fouad, he must avenge the murder."

"But…how would anyone know?" Rareburton asked. "I have said not a word to anyone about any oaths I've taken, not even to my family."

"There was another who knew about the oaths you took," Holmes said.

"But Fouad would not tell—"

"It would appear he did."

"He told you?" Rareburton asked his son.

Charles shook his head.

"Then who did he tell?"

"Me."

Everyone turned to the door. Standing at the threshold was Mrs. Rareburton clutching at her shawl. Her eyes were glistening with fresh tears.

"Mother!" cried Charles. "You shouldn't have followed me."

"I begged you not to come here, Charles. Why did you not listen?"

"Justina," the elder Rareburton said in a hoarse whisper. "What does this mean?"

"Pray come in, Madame," said Holmes. He gestured to a lone empty chair by the fireplace. "Will you not sit and tell us why you killed your relative?"

Mrs. Rareburton turned pale at Holmes' words and her bottom lip quivered. She took the chair he offered her, trembling and seemingly dazed at his revelation.

"Relative?" I repeated.

"Do you not see the resemblance about the eyes, Watson? And the accent."

"Sharif Fouad was my brother," Mrs. Rareburton admitted. She then sobbed into her handkerchief.

"I suspected as much. Mr. Fouad sought out your family, Mr. Rareburton, because you were married to his sister. A family relation is enough of a lure for someone seeking a new beginning. I fail to see why you did not tell me this, but it was almost clear to me from the moment I saw the victim."

Rareburton looked to his wife. "My wife asked that I not tell anyone of Mr. Fouad's relation to her."

"Sharif and I were orphans," Mrs. Rareburton added in a hoarse voice. "He and I were separated as small children. I never knew him during my childhood for I was raised in a convent orphanage. He was sent to a Coptic monastery, though he did not remain there. He discovered my link to him as an adult. I met Gerald while he was in Cairo because Sharif introduced me to him. But he asked that we not reveal our relation lest the Brotherhood use it to manipulate us."

"Then the question remains, why did you kill him?"

She looked up at my friend and a tear rolled down her cheek. "It was an accident. I was trying to stop him from hurting my son."

"And why was he hurting Charles?"

"I came to her defence," Charles said. "When I entered the store that morning he was yelling at my mother, threatening her. He had her by the arms and was shaking her."

"Oh good heavens," said Lestrade. "Will this ever end?"

"Of course, Lestrade," said Holmes. "As soon as Mrs. Rareburton informs us about the second Coptic patriarch."

Lestrade rolled his eyes. "What does that have to do with anything?"

"It is the point of everything, Lestrade," Holmes said. "Have you not been paying attention? The letter that was in Father Brown's pocket, the one that brought him to Fouad. That letter is at the root of this matter." Holmes turned to Mrs. Rareburton. "He told you about his letter."

"Yes."

"And did he tell you about the patriarch?"

She nodded. "Sharif said he'd met the patriarch in the monastery when they were boys. While Sharif left the monastery as soon as he was able, his friend took his final vows. But then he became involved with the local populace and joined the Brotherhood. He would funnel funds from the church into the Brotherhood and his own pockets. And just as they were about to suspect him, he converted to the Church of Rome. Sharif thought perhaps he saw the deeper pockets of Rome alluring."

"And with this letter to Brown, your brother had decided to betray him."

"I don't think he intended to betray him. He only wanted to warn his new associates of his duplicity. I don't think Sharif wanted harm to come to His Beatitude so much as for him to be called to repentance."

"Now, considering what your son witnessed when he walked into the store this morning, we can assume one of two things. Either Mr. Fouad feared you'd tell your husband of his plans with Brown, or he'd had second thoughts and didn't want you to say anything about what he'd told you."

She blinked up at him, apparently surprised that he'd deduced this. "It was the latter. He told me that if the patriarch was ruined, he might send people to find him. He'd become so frightened all of a sudden. I tried to calm him and tell him what he'd intended to do was the right thing, and suggested perhaps he should discuss it with Gerald, but he became irrational. He grabbed hold of me just as Charles arrived. Charles pulled him away from me, but then he fought back and started to choke my son. I snatched up the book to break his attention, to make him stop hurting Charles. But I—hit him in a bad spot." She choked out another deep sob and dabbed her eyes. "It was all so dreadful."

"Mother then sent me to call the Yard, which I did," said Charles. "She was going to turn herself over to the police. But when I returned, she remembered what my uncle had told her, that the closest member of the Brotherhood must avenge the murder one of his fellows."

"So your father would have to kill your mother and perhaps you for your involvement," Holmes said. "Then Father Brown arrived, and hearing from both of you what occurred and what it meant, he vowed to protect the two of you with the seal of the confessional."

"Blast," muttered Lestrade. He looked at Brown. "That's why you weren't talking."

"Why didn't I think of that?" Flambeau agreed.

"You were too close to the problem to see it," said Holmes.

"But the Rareburtons are not Catholic," said Lestrade.

"Oh no? Lestrade, look at what the lady is wearing around her neck." Holmes pointed to the silver oval pendant on a chain. "Do you not see it?"

"I thought it was some sort of coin," said Lestrade.

"A coin with an imprint of the Virgin Mary? Please, Lestrade. This is called a Miraculous Medal. I did a little research on these things a month ago with that murder of the nun near Tyburn. These medals are only worn in the Roman Church. The Coptic Church has no such tradition, therefore this woman is a Roman Catholic. And I'd surmise this is because the orphanage where she was raised was run by the Franciscans who are quite active in Alexandria and Cairo. Is that not so, Madame?"

"Yes."

"But her son is Anglican."

"It doesn't matter." Father Brown suddenly broke his silence in the corner. "She confessed to me and since he was part of that I could say nothing about the situation."

Lestrade sighed. "Well, I confess this is a bit more complicated than I thought." He unlocked the priest's handcuffs.

"Isn't it always?" I heard Holmes murmur.

Lestrade turned back to the

lady. "Madame, I must ask you to accompany me to the Yard. While Fouad's death was accidental, I must have a more thorough interview and an inquest must be arranged."

"The question remains, however," said Brown. "What will Mr. Rareburton do now?"

All eyes went to the gentleman who now sat with his head in his hand. He looked up and answered, "While I am a man of my word, I know that I cannot kill my own family. But when word of Fouad's death reaches Egypt, as I'm sure it will eventually with the public inquest, if I have done nothing to avenge Fouad they'll send people to take care of my family and me. To be honest, I don't know what to do."

Holmes went to his desk and pulled out a small packet of papers. He handed them to Rareburton.

"What are these?" He looked them over. "They're in Latin—identity papers from the Vatican?"

"And a letter of introduction from His Holiness allowing you entrance to any church property in all of Christendom. Monasteries, seminaries, convents. They will welcome you and your family."

"Where did you get these?"

"His Holiness provided me with them in 1891. In fact, I shall give you a letter of introduction so you might meet with the His Holiness personally to deliver Fouad's information regarding His Beatitude, if you are so inclined."

"The Pope would meet with us?"

"Of course he will."

"But I am Protestant."

"He has met with Protestants before, Mr. Rareburton." Holmes grinned. "As for the inquest, Dr. Watson, Monsieur Duroc, Father Brown, and I will take your part. It is best if you protect your family and become someone else living abroad. Your old friends should never find you."

After Lestrade left with the Rareburtons for Scotland Yard, Father Brown finally exited his corner to shake my friend's hand.

"Thank you, Mr. Holmes, for your assistance and for honouring my own vow of silence."

"It was my pleasure, Father Brown. But you should really thank your friend for bringing the case to me." He turned to Flambeau. "I trust you find all this satisfactory, Monsieur?"

"Very much, Mr. Holmes. I am grateful for your help and I would be overjoyed to pay you twice your regular fee—"

Holmes chuckled. "You want me to take some of the wealth you've stolen?"

"No, no, Mr. Holmes," Flambeau shook his head. "I am independently wealthy. I came from a good family who left me a sizable inheritance."

"Monsieur Duroc has also done his best to return what he could through circuitous means," said Father Brown. "And for what he could not return, he has donated money to the Church and other charities."

"Ah, very well then," said Holmes. "My standard fee is all I would require, no more. Though I must ask, Monsieur Duroc, what you plan to do with yourself now that you've abandoned your previous profession?"

Flambeau smiled. "I was thinking I might be a bit of a detective myself, though surely not one as accomplished as you and Father Brown. I thought as I know the secrets of thieves, I can use that against those who steal."

Holmes chuckled and shook his hand. "Quite reasonable. I hope you find the work rewarding."

One month later, Holmes accompanied Father Brown to meet with Cardinal Vaughn to serve as a witness regarding the matter of the Brown's incarceration. This meeting occurred in the midst of another problem that I have recorded for the public under the title "The Retired Colourman." As he thought it might be an involved meeting, Holmes sent me off to Lewisham to find evidence for the colourman case, and it was not until after the conclusion of that affair that I had the opportunity to ask Holmes what happened at the meeting with Cardinal Vaughn.

"I had to explain in detail the circumstances of the reverend father's imprisonment, the information on the patriarchs, and how I deduced what had transpired with particular regard to the seal of confession. When all that was done, His Eminence handed me a letter from His Holiness and asked, once I'd read it, if I'd mind sharing it with them. I did so, gladly. I have it here." He held up the letter with an elaborate red seal and handed it over to me. It was written in French, in a manner less formal than I'd seen him use in the past. The Pope's hand, I could see, while it had grown shaken with age, still allowed for clarity of the pen.

LEO PP. XIII

MY DEAR SON,

   I am eternally grateful to you for sending Mr. Gerald Rareburton and his family to me. The news his wife shared with me regarding His Beatitude Cyril II is disheartening. Unfortunately, as His Beatitude has already taken his position, there is little I can do about it at the present time. Nevertheless, due to your recommendation, I shall be vigilant with His Beatitude even while I accept him in charity. We shall leave word with Our successors that should he confirm suspicions, proper steps should be taken.*

   Mr. Rareburton has informed me of the danger his family faces in bringing me this information, so I am providing for their welfare. His son shall complete his education here in Rome. I've discovered that the young man has an interest in the work of my Cardinal Newman, which is most heartening.

   As always it warms my heart to hear from you. I pray you are well. Please give my fondest regards to your friend, Dr. Watson. As always, We render upon you and your friend our Apostolic blessing, and seek the intercession of the angels for all your intentions.

: *Leo P. P. XIII* :.

"I'm sure Monsieur Duroc will be pleased at the news," Holmes said.

"Speaking of Flambeau, Holmes, what do you plan to do about him?"

---

*Cyril II was "asked to leave" his position as Patriarch of the Coptic Catholic Church in 1904 over financial matters. He then joined the Greek Orthodox Church. The position of Patriarch of the Coptic Catholic Church was then left unfilled until the 1950s.

Holmes took his clay pipe from the mantle and filled it from the Persian slipper. "I shall do nothing."

"Nothing?"

"He has repented, has he not?"

"I wonder that he ever became a thief. If he already had money, why would he steal?"

"Because he could, Watson. Or because he was bored. There was a time in my life I may have contemplated such a career myself for similar reasons. Like Brown, on that subject, I too can understand a criminal soul." He lit his pipe and added, quietly. "I've acquired some respect for it, Watson."

"What, Holmes?"

"Faith. If it can change a hardened criminal like Flambeau, it is a powerful thing. His Holiness once said to me that it is rooted in human reason, and while I was dubious at the time, I've now come to agree that it is not an emotion. Nor is it irrational as I once believed it to be. It is quite the opposite, for it is what one knows to be true. His Holiness once wrote that 'God is not only true, He is Truth itself.' I do believe in Truth, Watson. A logician must believe in objective Truth, or there is nothing upon which one can base one's reasoning. And yet——" He took a puff from his pipe with a thoughtful expression. "It is a problem, Watson. A pretty little problem. Wouldn't you agree?"

ACKNOWLEDGMENTS

It is imperative that I thank so many people without whose assistance this book would never have come to be.

First, I must thank my husband Joseph Lewis for encouraging me to follow my calling as a writer and my son Raymond for understanding when Mommy is writing.

To those who have gone beyond, I thank Sir Arthur Conan Doyle for his unique creation Sherlock Holmes, G.K. Chesterton for penning the fantastic Father Brown, and His Holiness Pope Leo XIII for his inspiration.

Next, I would be remiss if I did not thank my critique partner in crime Karina Fabian, who never ceased to tell me what I needed to hear, as well as the following people who gave their thoughts on this work as it was being created: Dan Belford, Alexander Braun, Andrew Clark, Jim Clark, J. Thomas Crammond, David Downs, Karina Fabian, Grace Gallagher, Markus Harris, Father Geoffrey Horton, Philip K. Jones, AMS, Joshua Kenz, Ken Kirkman, Aaron and Jenifer Rosenberg, Steve Scott, Flora Spector, and Michael Tilden.

And finally, my heartfelt thanks to Steve Doyle, BSI and Mark Gagen, BSI for believing in *Murder in The Vatican*. You are the best.

—ANN MARGARET LEWIS

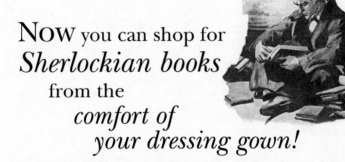